The Squirming

Jack Hamlyn

SEVERED PRESS
HOBART TASMANIA

The Squirming

WWW.SEVEREDPRESS.COM

ISBN: 978-1-925493-70-2

1

It was the little ones that bothered Kurta the most. The idea that there might be a tear in his hazmat suit and one of them would crawl inside and bore into him. That, more than anything, filled his guts with cold jelly and kept him awake far into the watches of night.

The others didn't know about that and he wasn't about to tell them. They weren't exactly the sensitive, compassionate types. At least on the surface. Underneath, of course, they were all terrified. Even Spengler and The Pole who had hearts like black ice. They all had their phobias and the greatest of them all was the idea of admitting to them.

"What's it gonna be, Kurt?" Spengler asked.

Kurta realized he'd been daydreaming again. The others stood around in their shiny green biosuits—*hotsuits* as they were known—awaiting his order. He looked from Spengler to Mooney to The Pole and West. Their faces were invisible behind the bubbles of their helmets and he was glad for that. They couldn't see him and he couldn't see them. Whatever they were thinking, he didn't know and none of them could see the anxiety etched into his face.

In front of them was another house in a row of them, all two-story clapboard, same design. Company houses. This one was painted green, the one next door blue.

"Same bit," he said. "Speng? You and The Pole go in the back way. We'll take the front. Call out when you're in position."

"Will do, Chief," Spengler said.

He led The Pole around the side through the uncut grass that came up above the ankles of their boots. Kurta stood there, waiting until they were in position while something in his guts went warm and runny. It was the middle of the afternoon and the sun was warm and bright. It gave him no sense of hope, no optimism. All he had to do was look around the neighborhood at all those houses lined up.

Jesus.

Once, people had lived here. They had fallen in love and raised families, watched their children playing on the green lawns and skipping up the sidewalks. They had marched their kids out trick-or-treating and shoveled snow and hung Christmas lights from the eaves and laughed as their sons and daughters lit off fireworks on warm Fourth of July evenings. The neighborhood had been alive and they lived with it, aged with it, grew old and content until the day came when life passed them by and they sat happily on their porches, no longer active participants, knowing they had done their best.

Now…now it was not a neighborhood.

It was a graveyard and the houses were tombstones. The only things that lived behind their walls were too horrible to contemplate, not human beings but pack animals, dumb beasts, mindless hosts caught in a dance of corruption with the crawling horrors that had enslaved them.

"Well?" West said. "We going in or what?"

Ah, young and stupid, bite your tongue.

Kurta almost laughed at his naïveté.

Poor, silly little puppy. Testosterone primed, adrenaline juicing, full of the kill-happy military brainwashing that got a lot of boys bagged in a lot of wars.

West was new.

He'd only been with the unit three days. He'd seen some minor league slugification yesterday, but today was the day when he'd wade through it, hip-deep in human wreckage. Then he wouldn't be so goddamn anxious.

He replaced Stiv whom Kurta liked a lot. A punk rock, edgy, narcissistic asshole that wiped his ass with the flag, Stiv had been young and tough. Anytime somebody saluted Kurta—something Kurta hated with a passion—Stiv would unzip his pants and give a counter-salute with his dick. That drove the patriotic lemmings shit-crazy which made Stiv laugh all that much harder.

Inside his helmet, Kurta frowned.

Stiv was gone now. He'd gotten blown away accidentally as he rescued The Pole and Mooney who'd been besieged by a gang of randy slugheads. Spengler had done it. He lost his nerve and opened up. Friendly fire. Something Kurta would never let him forget, G.I. Joe Spengler whose old man had been a full colonel in the Marines before the good old U S of fucking A had dropped its pants, bent over, and got sodomized by the slugs.

Now there was no Marines, no Army, no Navy, nothing but a ragtag collection of exterminators (as they were known), trying to quell the infestation. Town to town, house to house to house.

It's a fucking joke, Stiv used to tell the newbies. *Like the old days, War on Terror and all that—a waste of time. We ain't stopping the slugs any more than we stopped the extremists. All the bullets and firepower couldn't change the way those pricks thought, and we can't stop the slugs from breeding. That's what nature designed them to do. They eat, they fuck, they enslave us.*

Kurta sighed. *Goddamn Stiv.*

West was getting excited and Kurta could feel it. Mooney said that Spengler and The Pole had breached the back door. They were calling on the headset.

"Well?" West said again.

Kurta nodded. "Okay, let's do this. Moon, take the point." He tried to say this authoritatively like some old school dipfuck of the Chuck Norris variety. Inside, he felt a lot more like Don Knotts.

2

"On your right," Kurta called over the headset.

Mooney dropped back, tripped over his own boots in his clumsy biosuit and went down on his ass.

The slughead came waltzing down the stairs, hissing and gnashing his yellow teeth, his contorted face a bad Halloween mask that was melting like wax. He was pregger, all right, one arm cradling his swollen parasite in its webby flesh-sling. He would mother that horror until there was nothing left of him and the slug molted into something worse.

West panicked, opening up with his M4 and stitching the ceiling with rounds. Kurta cursed under his breath, shoved West aside, and blasted the slughead with his riot gun, giving him two rounds point blank.

It got ugly then.

The slughead was nearly cut in half, gushing fluids and slug-slime, legs wanting to go one way while his torso tried to go the other. The whole time, he was thrashing and jerking violently, his organs spilled down the stairs, a knob of spine poking out of his back like a snapped broomstick.

"GYAAAHHHHH!" he squealed.

"GYAAAAAAHHHHHHGG—"

In the process, a rat from a sinking ship (in this case, one that was horribly staved-in and bilged), the slug emerged from its protective sling. It was about seven inches long, looking oddly like some well-greased swollen phallus, fleshy and spouting copious amounts of lucite-clear gunk. Its gestation had been interrupted and it wasn't too happy about it. Its head split open in a star-shaped mouth which spat a glob of phlegm at West that missed and struck the wall. Immediately, it attached itself to the paneling, sprouting wiry tendrils that juiced the veneer with neurotoxins.

"Burn it!" Kurta said over the headset. "Goddammit, Mooney, you fucktard! Burn it!"

Mooney was on his feet by then. He brought the gun of the flamethrower up and it gushed out a tongue of burning napalm that engulfed the slughead and his attendant parasite. The slughead writhed for a few seconds and then went still, burning and popping.

Kurta held up a gloved hand, counting off, *one, two, three, four*—

"Okay, West," he said. "Hose him down."

West shakily stepped forward. He wore a backpack similar to the flamethrower except his tanks were filled with a Halogen derivative. He aimed the hose at the fire and the foamy white chemical extinguished the flames on contact.

He turned back towards Kurta. "Guess…guess I fucked up back there."

"Don't worry about it," Kurta reassured him.

On the stairs, there were only blackened remains glistening with white foam now. They used to use an acid composite, but it was hard to get these days so they went back to the old flamethrowers. They worked, but they created an ugly mess. The remains were still smoking. Now and again, something would pop like a coal in a campfire.

Kurta was glad he had a mask on so he didn't have to smell the stink.

There was gunfire from the back of the house.

"You got some?" he asked over the headset.

"Two of 'em," The Pole said. "And pretty fucking randy. Spengler is toasting 'em. Get the kid back here or this place'll go up."

"You heard 'em," Kurta said. "Go with him, Moon."

Mooney led West towards the back of the house and Kurta stood there alone, wondering what kind of shit they were going to get into upstairs. He hated houses because the rooms were small and the hallways narrow. It was easy to get bottled-up in them. Buildings were better: bigger rooms, bigger corridors.

He looked around.

The house was dim, shadowy, claustrophobic. He didn't like it. In fact, it made his scalp crawl inside his helmet.
Hell was that?

Not from above. Over beyond the stairs. Sure, he hadn't seen it when they first came in but there was a doorway there, an archway really, that led into a dining room maybe. He knew he should have waited for the team, but, hell, the sooner they cleaned this house out, the sooner they could get back to the bunker and get loaded.

There was inspiration in that.

Swallowing, his Ithaca 37 riot gun raised, tactical light on it peeling back the shadows, he waited for something to spring out at him, but there was nothing.

He moved quietly, sweating inside his suit. His mouth was dry. His instincts were sharp, hot pins inside him.
The archway.

He panned his light over it, saw nothing that worried him. Okay. The archway didn't lead into a dining room as he thought; there was a set of steps beyond it leading down into the darkness. The basement. The steps were carpeted. Probably a rec room down there with a bar and pool table. A man cave.

The question was: did he go down alone?
Chances were, there'd be nothing down there, but you never really knew. The fool hero thing was to go down alone. His

skin crawled at the idea. His imagination gave him a little tour of Hell in which dozens of slugheads came charging out at him, burying him in their numbers.

No, he would wait.

It was the reasonable thing to do.

He heard a bumping and thumping sound above. There was someone up there. Slugheads were too stupid for stealth, their brains gone to Silly Putty.

"We're coming in," Mooney said.

It was important to announce your presence when there was an exterminator with his finger on the trigger. The tendency to shoot first was a given when slugheads were around.

Mooney showed with West in tow. The Pole and Spengler filed in behind them.

"Okay," Kurta told them. "I heard someone moving upstairs and someone, I think, down below. Spengler, you and The Pole go upstairs. Moon, you go with them. Don't bunch up. West? You're with me."

The Pole led the way up the stairs. Spengler waited until he was half way up before he started after him. Then Mooney followed.

"All right, kid," Kurta said. "Stay with me."

"Okay."

Kurta noticed that he didn't sound quite so anxious now. There was something about your first real contact with the enemy that took the stuffing out of you.

3

There was no handrail, so Kurta moved slowly down the carpeted steps. He didn't like carpeting under his boots; he liked good old wood. Carpeting got slippery. So he moved very carefully.

At the bottom, he paused, scanning about with his light. Sure, it was just as he thought. A rec room spread out before him. There was even a bar and the obligatory pool table. A sofa, a few chairs. An antique Pac-Man arcade game in the corner, dartboard on the wall. Old Spuds MacKenzie mirrors on the wall. Very 1980s, very retro.

"Hang back until I tell you different," he told West.

He stepped away from the stairs. This was going to be a bust. At least, he hoped it would be. The thing he didn't like was all the shadows. He wished he had some night-vision gear, but it was hard to get these days. When Supply got some, he'd probably get three pairs. That's how they worked. Feast or famine. When he requisitioned a new pair of boots, they sent him a pair and an extra boot. What the hell was he supposed to do with one right boot and two left ones? They think he had three feet?

Over beyond the bar, there was another doorway. Maybe a junk room or a bedroom. He moved to the side to look behind the couch and a slughead stepped out of the corner, growling and gurgling. His eyes were like juicy pink scabs.

"Shit," Kurta said under his breath, backing away.

The slughead, nursing its parasite as they did with one hand, charged. It wasn't that he saw Kurta as the enemy so much as he saw him as food. Anything that walked, hopped, skittered, or crawled was food to them. That was their job. As host to the slugs, they had to keep them well-fed so their appetites were voracious.

Kurta fired.

The slughead's face went to hamburger, his teeth scattering across the bar top. He spun around in a circle. It looked like he was going down, then, at the last possible moment, he changed trajectory.

He leaped out at Kurta.

Kurta fired, but the slughead's hand knocked the barrel aside and the buckshot shattered a Spuds MacKenzie from its hook. The slughead rammed into Kurta and knocked him on his ass. Bleeding and groaning, his face hanging from a thread like a particularly rancid cutlet, he aimed a wild kick and caught Kurta in the helmet.

Then West fired, drilling six rounds into him.

He jerked with the impact, going down, his loose, meaty face slapping off the felt of the pool table in his downward descent, leaving a greasy smear.

"Nice shooting," Kurta said.

Something slithered up his hotsuit and he realized it was the guy's slug free from its sling. It inched up his leg and he smashed it with the butt of the riot gun again and again until it let go and dropped to the floor, squirming and leaking a foul brown juice like the blood of a spider. He brought his boot down on it, smashing it to a pool of viscous goo. It made a sort of high-pitched whirring sound as it died.

The Pole came over the headset, wanting to know what was going on and if they needed backup.

"We just greased a slughead," Kurta explained. "We got this—"

Then West let out a cry that was half-terror and half-surprise. Kurta swung around, bringing his light to bear and five or six slugheads came surging out of the back room, fluid and dark and menacing.

West opened up, capping slugs into them.

He hit three of them, ripped some holes in the wall, but that was about it. The slugheads kept coming. Without proper headshots to drop them, they were nearly unstoppable, Kurta knew. Even missing limbs would not slow them because their parasites wanted meat and the hosts lived only to provide it.

West was practically screaming over the headset: "THEY'RE EVERYWHERE! SLUGGOS FUCKING EVERYWHERE!"

As Kurta started popping rounds from the riot gun, he wasn't honestly sure what he was more afraid of—the slugheads or West's shooting.

One of the slugheads made it around the pool table. He was a large man, though emaciated as they all were from the slugs sucking the nutrients out of them. His slug was particularly huge, riding in its sling against his belly like an especially fat summer sausage. The guy clawed out, pink and white foam bubbling from his mouth in stringy gouts.

"Eyuuuuughllll," was about the best he could do for speech.

Kurta gave it to him at close range.

His head exploded like a pus-filled boil, soggy gray matter and skull fragments spattering against the walls and ceiling. He hit the floor, jumping and jerking.

His slug emerged from its sling immediately, shearing through the gauzy flesh like a python bursting through rotten wicker.

It coiled on the floor.

It located a host immediately and wasted no time in procuring it. It convulsed and spat a gob at Kurta who wasn't fast enough to get away. The gob splatted against the bubble of his helmet, wiry tendrils trying to dig into the Acrylite and inject a brain cocktail that would drop him to his knees where he would happily pick up Mr. Slug and attach him to his soft white underbelly.

Fuck that.

Kurta blasted it to sauce, brushed the gob away, and began firing in the direction of the massing slugheads. West dropped one of them with a headshot when he was mere feet from Kurta, blood and brain goo splattering against Kurta's bubble, blinding him.

Jesus!

He tried to wipe it clear with his sleeve, but he only managed to smear it into a paste-like emulsion. He fought blind, firing in the direction of the slugheads, screaming out for backup. When his riot gun was empty, he swung it like a club, feeling it mashing into soft faces and splintering bone.

He fell back, knowing he was in the shit, stumbling back towards the bar, guided by the light bars on his helmet. He grabbed the first bottle he found which was Absolut vodka and poured it right over his bubble. The alcohol dissolved the brain emulsion and the vodka washed away the mess.

He saw West in some kind of hand-to-hand battle with a slughead. He was punching his attacker in the face with the awful, soft sound of a fist sinking into a rotting pumpkin. The slughead had both hands on his helmet and it looked as if he was trying to pull it off.

Kurta pulled the .357 Colt Python from its holster on his web belt and blew the slughead's noggin almost entirely from his neck. Blood sprayed over West's faceshield, but it was better than the alternative.

By then, another one was coming at Kurta.

He fired wildly, missing sluggo's head and punching a fist-sized hole in his throat. He went down and Kurta kicked him the face. It was like sponge cake and exploded off the skull beneath. Another round finished him.

Kurta turned and one of them rocketed out of the darkness and tackled him. He hit the floor, the .357 flying from his grip.

The slughead straddling him was a woman with a face like bleeding suet, loose and dangling from the bone. He fought against her, but it wasn't so easy in his cumbersome biosuit. She was frenzied, absolutely demented, and viciously determined.

She gripped his helmet and banged it off the floor again and again, grinding her hips against him. Ribbons of pus dripped from holes in her face onto the glass. Then she brought her mouth down against the bubble and began licking it, leaving a trail of pink juice over it.

Kurta reached down and found his knife, fumbling it from its sheath as the woman licked and sucked at his bubble. He nearly dropped it, then got it in his fist, and brought it to bear, stabbing her in the throat again and again until she pulled away, shrieking. She gripped her head with both hands as if she was afraid it might come apart if she didn't.

With a cry, he jabbed the blade into her left eye socket, the orb splashing free from its housing in a slime of optic tissue. Howling with lunacy, she grabbed his hand and only succeeded in drawing the blade downward, splitting her face in half. Gouts of gore splashed against his bubble.

Then her head exploded.

Spengler and Mooney were in the room, driving the remaining slugheads back and down with sustained fire. The Pole had West and he was dragging him up the stairs.

Something which was not easy because West was fighting against him, completely out of his head by that point.

Kurta pulled back, and Mooney hosed the room down with his flamethrower until everything was burning.

By the time they made it out onto the lawn, the entire house was blazing.

"Good thing is," The Pole said, "weren't no sluggos upstairs. Nothing but a dog. A big old mangy retriever."

"You shoulda seen it, boss," Mooney said. "Fucking dog was infested. He had three slugs on him. Most pathetic thing I ever saw."

"What did you do with it?" Kurta asked.

"I wasted it," Spengler said. "Couldn't leave it like that. What if it was your dog?"

4

Back at the APC, they hosed each other down with wormicide from the sprayer that killed any nasty parasites or dangerous microorganisms on contact. It stank like bleach (which was its active ingredient), but it did the job. After a few moments, they took their helmets off. It was nice to feel the fresh air, though in that neighborhood there was a certain smell of decay that was ever-present.

Pulling off a cigarette, Kurta said, "You okay, kid?"

West was sitting on the curb, a blank look in his eyes. "I really fucked up, didn't I?"

"Nah," Mooney told him. "It happens to everyone."

"There were so many of 'em...I just, I don't know, I guess I kinda froze at the end there."

"You did fine," Kurta said.

"Really?" West brightened.

"Sure."

The Pole lit a cigarette off the butt of his last. "Next time I try to save your ass, cherry, don't fight me or I'll leave you. I got better things to do than nipple-feed you."

"Go easy," Mooney said.

"Fuck that. Did you see how this little prick fought me? He pulls that girly shit on me again and he ain't gonna like how it turns out."

"Shut the fuck up," Kurta told him.

The Pole didn't like being talked to like that.

His eyes were full of acid as he stared at Kurta. Kurta met his gaze, held it, dared him to take it farther. The Pole didn't. As team leader, Kurta owned his ass and he knew it. It all came down to necessity. If The Pole wanted to stay on the team, then he had to keep on Kurta's good side. That way he ate good back at the bunker, had access to good liquor and weed, a roof over his head, protection, and sometimes even girls. He pissed Kurta off, he'd be demoted, end up on one of the scavenging crews or waste disposal, picking up corpses in the streets or work animal control putting down the roving packs of wild dogs. There were other jobs like medical and food service, but a guy like The Pole wouldn't rate them without training. And schools were real hard to come by these days.

"Sure, boss," he finally said, grinning with his bad teeth.

Kurta didn't even bother commenting on that.

Time was going to come, he knew, when he and The Pole were going to go head to head. Had to happen. The Pole was always going out of his way to question Kurta's authority. Kurta put up with it for team unity. He always wanted his boys to chip in if they had a better plan than the one he came up with. Problem was, The Pole took it too far. He always had to keep pushing, see how far he could get.

Keep it up, Kurta thought, *just keep it up. Won't be a fucking demotion for you, dipshit. You'll get left behind with the slugs.*

He pushed that from his mind because he didn't need any more negativity blowing through his head than he already had. He sat there, pulling off his smoke, watching the house burn. If it was up to him, he would burn them all flat, town after town after town. That way, you could be sure the slug infestation would be eradicated.

But command didn't want that.

They wanted the houses cleared one by one because some day (they claimed with rosy, self-deluding optimism), people would be moving back into those neighborhoods which would be the anchors of productive, self-sustaining communities.

Kurta laughed dryly and butted out his cigarette.

Spengler had a pint of Jim Beam and he was passing it around. Kurta was okay with that. A good snort now and again steeled a man and ironed out his nerves so they weren't bent like pins.

"The crazy, crazy shit you see," Spengler said as the bottle made the rounds, spirits buoyed. "I was in this house, Northside Cleveland. We had it cleared out except for the attic. I go up there and this sluggo comes crawling out of the dark. Old lady, had to been pushing eighty. I open up, peel the top of her head off and...*Jesus*...I can see right inside her skull and it looks like a Cup o' Noodles in there with all slugs squirming in her brain."

The Pole laughed, then grimaced at the very idea of it.

"Those weren't slugs," Mooney pointed out. "They were flukes, parasitic flatworms. The slugs carry them like cattle carry liver flukes. Once a slug parasitizes a host, it releases larval flukes which migrate immediately to the brain."

Sometimes they forgot that Mooney had taught high school biology once. Regardless, it led to a lively discussion of the life cycle of the slugs (which still wasn't completely understood), from the larval stage ("wigglers") to the adult slugs to the final molting which produced leggy horrors known as "creepers." Mooney pointed out that it was the flukes that hijacked human beings, making them slaves of the slugs.

It was a weird symbiosis.

Somehow, the flukes were servitors of the slugs. When they entered their host, they released an endorphin cocktail which overloaded the human nervous system, creating an overdosing pleasure response which pretty much turned humans into addicted zombies.

Scientifically, it was very similar to heroin addiction. In the central part of the human brain known as the basal forebrain, there was a cluster of nerve cells known as the nucleus accumbens, which was an integral part of the reward circuit which was activated by massive doses of dopamine during sex, eating rich food, or taking drugs. The flukes mimicked this, flooding the nervous system with neurotransmitters, creating a "high" of the sort associated with heroin. This surge literally exhausted the nerve cells from constant stimulation, so the brain dampened the dopamine response as it did with opiate addicts. The end result was that the hosts needed more and more of a *hit* from the flukes to trigger the same dopamine response. So, essentially, the slugheads were addicts. They would do anything to please the flukes which in turn existed to please the slug itself. And *anything* meant eating and eating, stuffing themselves with meat which provided the slugs with the proteins they craved.

Any meat.

Which turned them into cannibalistic monsters whose brains were turned to sludge from fluke infestations. The life of the host was a matter of months at best.

"That's what I don't get," The Pole said. "Why the fuck are we doing this? Why don't we just let the sluggos die off and be done with it?"

"Because the slugs are aggressive. They are not going to simply stop...not until the last potential hosts are exhausted and the life cycle ceases," Mooney pointed out.

"Sure," Spengler said, "which means the extinction of the human race."

"All mammals for that matter," Mooney added.

The addiction thing fascinated Kurta.

As a guy who'd spent two years spiking junk before he was arrested and detoxed, he understood addiction. With the slugs, the addiction cycle began when they spat those globs at people which juiced them with endorphins, triggering opiate receptors in the brain and creating a joyous analgesic effect. The perfect little high which lasted only seconds. The only way to get more was to pick up the slug and place it against your belly…and your brain instinctively understood that.

Once you did that, there was no going back because the flukes entered your system upon contact.

Fascinating, all right.

As the others chatted away, Kurta sat there with West.

You were in the Guards before this, weren't you, kid?"

West nodded. "Three years. Then everything went to shit and there were no more Guards. I had a girl. We were saving up to buy a house…then, well, you know."

Kurta sighed. "Yeah, I know."

"How long you been doing this?"

"Over a year now."

"God, that's a long time."

"Sure."

"Why do you keep at it?"

Kurta shrugged. "I ask myself that every day. Still don't have an answer. Guess I do it because it has to be done. You know your dad?"

West was taken aback by that. "Um…sure. He was great. Died of a heart attack before the slugs came. That's a blessing."

"What did he do?"

"Dad? He worked in a foundry. An awful place, hot and stinking. He'd come home every night exhausted, dirty. He'd barely finish his supper before he fell asleep. But he took good care of us. He always took good care of us. Lots of food. Clothes on our backs. Toys. Bikes. Summer camps. You name it. He made sure we had it."

Kurta smiled. "You know why he did that, kid? Because it was the right thing to do. My old man worked in a foundry, too. I know what that's about. It's a fucking shit job. Your old man hated it, I bet, like my old man did, but he did it because he didn't have choices in life like some people. He did it because he loved you. He did it because it was the right thing to do and he wanted you to have a better life than he had."

"I guess you're right, Kurt."

"Course I'm right. Remember that: I'm always right. You do that and we'll get along fine, you and me."

A chopper buzzed high overhead, then circled back around once, then twice.

"Uh-oh," Mooney said.

"What?" West asked.

"It's the fucking major," Spengler said.

A call came in on the radio and Kurta, sighing, climbed into the APC to take it. "This is Ex-Three, over."

"OVER, MY ASS!" a voice screamed over the band.

"GODDAMMIT, KURTA! WHAT THE FUCK ARE YOU STUPID JACKASSED MOTHERFUCKING MORONS DOING DOWN THERE? HAVING A FUCKING WEENIE ROAST? WHY IS THAT STRUCTURE BURNING? YOU KNOW THE GODDAMN RULES! NO HOUSES ARE BURNT DOWN, YOU FUCKING MONKEYSKULL!"

"Yes, sir," Kurta said. "I know the rules, sir."

"THEN WHY THE FUCK IS THAT STRUCTURE BURNING?"

"Collateral damage, sir. Collateral damage."

5

The bunker.

Three stories of reinforced concrete and steel, one level above ground and two below. It was guarded by tire traps and cement berms and a twelve-foot chain-link fence that encircled the compound. Shooters with night-vision scopes watched the outer perimeter. They had .30 cal sniper rifles and .50 cal machine guns at their disposal. The bunker sat dead-center, or nearly, of Lorrain Air National Guard Base. It was designed during the Cold War to house those who were *not* expendable in the case of a nuclear war—politicians, dignitaries, high-ranking Air Force staff and assorted technicians. It was made to accommodate a hundred people and to accommodate them in comfort with private sleeping quarters, gyms, recreation rooms, meeting rooms and war rooms, medical and laboratory facilities, plus enough food and water to last five years after the fresh stuff ran out.

There were currently some fifty-odd people in the bunker. It had been in operation just over a year and each month, two or three others came in. The place was operated by Dr. Dewarvis, a former CDC parasitologist, but actually run by Major Trucks who was in charge of security.

To the south, there had been three other *doom bunkers* (as they were called) at Wright-Patterson AFB. But only one was currently in operation; the other two had been shut down because of slug outbreaks. Which was a dread that everyone lived with on a daily basis. They were trying to survive against an adversary that nature had designed to inherit the earth. They told themselves that they would win in the end, but nobody really believed that. Oh, they told the children that there was no real danger but when the kids weren't around, the forecast was exceedingly grim.

As the country had discovered more than once, there were some wars you simply couldn't win.

6

While the others socialized and drank and smoked weed, Kurta stayed to himself. They were blowing off steam. He understood the need; he just couldn't be part of it. His good times were long ago.

He laid there in his bed, staring at the battleship-gray walls and pulling off a cigarette, thinking, remembering, punishing himself with guilt because that's what he was good at.

He thought about the Army.

He'd pulled six years before the trouble started, before he fell in with the wrong people in Thailand and hanged himself. The Army didn't look kindly at him trafficking narcotics. The only thing that really saved him from a ten- to twenty-year stretch at Leavenworth was public perception. The Army was real sensitive about it. They liked to control it. Manipulate it. And what they didn't want was their soldiers going on trial for heroin trafficking. When the people back home found out that there was a U.S. Army narcotics ring operating out of Asia, the shock waves would be heard in Washington and things would get ugly in the Far East Command. So, they cut Kurta and the others a deal— dishonorable discharge, six months in the brig, then out.

They all took what was offered.

This was the first of what Kurta liked to think of as his BIG FUCKUPS.

The second one was even worse. He bumped around for awhile, taking one job after another: driving truck, working in a bakery, crewing a fishing boat. He worked hard, went to school at night, got his welding certificate. Good jobs were easy to come by then. He met Pammy, fell in love, got married, and they had Lucy. Everything was right. He was pulling twelve-hour days, so Pammy took care of everything. She ran the house, she paid the bills, raised Lucy. She made great meals that didn't come out of a box or a can. He was happy. But through it all, as good as things were, he felt the urge to run wild again. Before long, he was running with his old crew from high school, selling weed and then junk— because that's where the money was. He kept telling himself that he'd get out, but by then he was snorting heroin and, soon enough, shooting it. Another junkie pushing drugs to support his habit. He lost his job, was put through detox twice. That's when Pammy left him. She couldn't take it anymore. She was tired of lying to her own daughter when Lucy asked why daddy was sick all the time.

Kurta lost everything.

That was the second—and biggest—of his BIG FUCKUPS.

By the time he straightened out, the slugs came. They got both of his girls and that was that. He'd been alone since.

As he butted his cigarette and pulled off a can of beer, he thought, *the slugs, those fucking slugs.*

Nobody knew what their origin was. Not really. The infestation swept the globe and something like 80% of the human race was infected within two months. People said it was the result of Russian genetic engineering. They claimed it was a terrorist plot financed by radical Islam. They said the slugs were a synthetic organism that escaped from a U.S. transgenics lab. Others claimed that the slugs arose from nature—all the toxins we'd been dumping into the soil and water for decades had given birth to a new and deadly life form. Mother Nature was kicking our asses for polluting and poisoning the Eden that she'd given us. Still others were certain the slugs had come from outer space.

In the end, nobody really knew.

The experts said they were not the end result of biotechnology and Frankenscience run wild. Manufactured organisms were easily detectable in the lab. And the slugs had the same DNA as every other living thing on earth, so that ruled out the idea that they came from Mars or Altair 4. Chances were, the biogenetics and evolutionary biology people said, they were a very successful mutation, possibly created or enhanced via man-made pollutants.

Nobody knew for sure.

Save the slugs and they weren't saying.

"And now the human race is spam in a fucking can," Kurta said out loud. "Way past our freshness date. Next stop, extinction."

It should have frightened him, but it didn't.

Mankind had been asking for this for years and now here it was.

7

Back at it.

Kurta led Ex-3, as Extermination Team #3 was known, down into the moldering cellars of an apartment building on West 27th. They'd been at it all morning, cleaning out floor after floor after floor. They'd been issued new biosuits, white Tyvek full containment suits, because the old ones were starting to smell pretty bad and the seams were getting worn. It only took one little hole for a wiggler to breach a suit. The new Tyveks were lighter, cooler, but the choice of color was a really bad idea. By the time Kurta and the boys got down to the cellar, they were stained with gore, spattered with tissue and vomit, bile and blood, all manner of assorted drainage.

They fanned out in the cellar, went through it room by room, but there was nothing.

"I'd say this is a done deal," Mooney said over the headset. "Let's get the hell out of here."

"I'm all for that," The Pole said.

"What about the tunnels?" West asked.

"Jesus Christ," Spengler said. "I ain't going in there. No fucking way am I going in there."

The Pole swore under his breath. "Yeah, shut your hole, punk."

Kurta stood there, thinking.

He could hear the hiss of the team's respirator masks. The kid was right. There were steam tunnels connecting most of the buildings on the block. Perfect hiding places for slugheads. Down in the moist darkness was the perfect place to find nests. Nobody wanted to go in there, but Kurta didn't see where they had a choice.

"We need to clean them out," he announced.

Spengler turned on West. "Good going, shit-fer-brains. You want the tunnels? Good, you can lead the way in."

The Pole shoved West out of the way.

"Well, isn't that what we're here for?" West asked.

"I suggest you shut your mouth now," The Pole threatened.

"We could have been out of here if it wasn't for you and your big fucking mouth."

"Oh, I'll remember this, kid," Spengler said.

Kurta stiffened inside his suit. "That'll do. He's right and you know he's right."

Still cursing the very idea, The Pole led the way to the steam tunnels. They panned the opening with their lights. The passage went on farther than their beams would reach, a claustrophobic space of clutching shadows about five feet wide and maybe seven in height. Steam pipes and electrical conduits ran along the walls, data and telephone lines strung between them.

"Here's your chance, kid," Spengler said. "You can be the big man now. Show us how good your nerves are."

"No," Kurta said. "The kid is with me. *You* got point, Speng."

"Fuck that! I'm not going in there!"

"Yes, you are, hero. You're going to lead us in," Kurta told him. "Remember how Stiv used to lead us in, Speng? Remember that, *hero?* Remember how he'd volunteer every time? He had balls. Something you don't have. So, yes, you're on point. In fact, I think you should be on point for a long time. Do it for the team and do it for Stiv…okay, *hero?*"

There were a few moments of tense silence and Kurta just waited for it. Waited for Spengler to mouth off. Because when he did, he was going to beat his ass senseless and hand-feed him to the first drooling sluggo he met.

But all Spengler did was say, "Yes, sir," in a very mousy voice.

Without further prompting, he led the way in. The Pole went next, then Kurta and West, finally Mooney who watched the back door as always because Kurta didn't trust Spengler or The Pole behind him with loaded weapons.

8

They kept five or six feet between them so that they had fighting room in case things got ugly. Spengler moved forward very slowly, sweeping his Ithaca 37 pump back and forth. The tactical light bracketed to the rail atop it cast wild, darting shadows before him. He was trying real hard not to let what Kurta said rattle him. The time would come when the score was evened. But that time wasn't now, so he didn't waste mental energy on it.

Fucking prick, he just won't let the thing about Stiv die. He just can't let it go.

"Shut up," he said under his breath.

The headset caught it and The Pole said, "What?"

"Nothing."

"Eyes up and mouths shut," he heard Kurta say.

Sure, asshole, you can count on me.

Spengler moved cautiously forward, just ready for the shit because when you were an exterminator, shit was your natural element: you learned to live in it, wade through it, and recognize its smell when you were about to step in it.

"Wait," he said.

"Something?" Kurta asked.

"Thought I saw a shadow move up there…pull away from the light." He paused, uncertain. "Hang back. I'm going to go forward."

The others pulled back.

"Watch yourself," Kurta said.

Spengler didn't bother commenting on that because he knew damn well that fucking Kurta relished the idea of his death.

Swallowing, he let his instincts guide him forward. Yes, there it was again…something moving just ahead, trying to avoid the light. He moved faster now and saw a shambling figure trying to escape the seeking beam. They were clinging to the wall, pulling themselves forward with the steam pipes. It was a man.

Or something like a man. He was hunched over, back to Spengler. A big guy in a black leather motorcycle jacket that was shiny like the shell of a beetle. It was split open in numerous places, and Spengler could see a mutiny of flesh poking out, viscid and bubbly.

"Hey, shithead," Spengler said.

The figure turned and faced him.

He made a moaning/groaning sound and his voice had a creaky, rusty sound to it as he mumbled typical sluggo gibberish. His face was blown up, rearranged, drawn and twisted, a veritable seething puzzlebox of disease and rot, gashes and hollows and flaccid folds of skin like tiny balloons. One graying eye was filmed and sightless, rolling in its socket like a grub in an egg sac, staring up at the ceiling. The other was simply gone.

"What do you got?" The Pole asked.

"Nothing yet. Hang tight," Spengler told him. He had something, all right, but he just wasn't sure what. Whatever it was, he hadn't seen it before, and his curiosity was aroused.

He got in closer, but still maintained an easy ten feet between himself and his quarry. This slughead looked like he was all done in. Still, you never knew. They could be fast when they wanted to stuff themselves with meat. Yet,

Spengler didn't think this one was interested in eating; it was up to something else and that's what intrigued him and piqued his morbid curiosity.

The sluggo leaned there against the wall, breathing with a loud rattling sound as if his lungs were filled with metal shards and old razor blades. His mouth was a ragged aperture like the cut from a dull ax. Every time he sucked in a wheezing, scraping breath, a sort of pink slime dripped from his mouth. And judging from the globby accumulated crust down his bare chest, he had been doing that for some time.

What intrigued Spengler the most was that this sluggo did not want to reveal his rider, the slug that was attached to his belly. He was trying to cover it with his jacket, both hands cradling the bulge like a woman in her ninth month cradling the child in her belly.

Show me. Show me what you got. Because if it's what I think it is, things are definitely looking up.

The sluggo made no threatening moves. He was like some sick animal that just wanted to crawl away and die in peace. But Spengler was not about to let him crawl away. Not now. Not with what was under his hands.

The others were calling, wanting to know what was going on, but Spengler ignored them. He jabbed the barrel of his Ithaca forward and it had the intended result. The sluggo hissed and clawed out in the vague direction of the barrel and when he did so, Spengler put the light on his belly and...*holy Jesus, would you fucking look at that?* Old Speng had been in the extermination game for some time but he'd never seen one of these. Kurta had more than once, but never him.

This was it.

This was the thing, baby.

"I got one," he said, eyeing the obscenely swollen mass at the sluggo's belly. It was like some horrendous externalized placenta, threaded right into the sluggo's wasted anatomy by elastic strings of tissue. The slug hung there in its flesh-sling like a swollen, fat little loaf of Vienna bread. He could see it squirming in the sheath which was a leprous, transparent yellow like piss-stained waterproof plastic, pulsating and veined purple.

Poor old slughead, he was just about done in—like a living rack of crow-picked bones, a breathing, hissing carcass that was leaking fluids and pissing corpse gas. His skin had the consistency of watery tapioca, dripping and oozing at his feet in glops of flesh-slag. It hung from his face like blood-stained bandages. His body contorted and jerked like a rat full of strychnine. His torso looked as if it was beginning to split open. His boots skidded in the pool of drainage he was creating, one arm looped around a steam pipe, the other holding the slug-sling.

"Up here!" Spengler called over the headset. "I think...I think I got a fucking creeper! Get your asses up here now!"

There was a lot of squawking coming over the headset now. Back at the bunker, the techies and labcoat johnnies wanted all the creepers they could get their forceps on. For Spengler, it meant an automatic bump in pay and plenty of benefits like good booze, better food, maybe even a girl.

Hot damn!

But he had to secure the little monster first and its host, as damaged and drained as he was, wasn't going to stand still to see his "baby" fall into uncaring hands.

With a sudden violent cry that became a shrill, ungodly howling that echoed like a jackhammer in the closeness of the tunnel, he launched himself at Spengler.

But Spengler kept his cool.

There was too much on the line not to.

When the sluggo jumped, he jerked the trigger on his Ithaca 37, racked the pump, and fired again.

The sluggo never had a chance.

The top of his head took the first shot. It vaporized into a blood mist of mucilage that painted the steam pipes a glistening red. Clots of tissue were mixed in with it and they writhed like maggots…except they weren't maggots, of course, but the flukes that had hot-wired his brain. The second shot erased his face and what was left of his head flew apart in a red-pink-gray eruption of skull-bone and flesh that sprayed against the wall.

Spengler was certain that the sluggo's filmed eye hit the wall like a juicy grape.

By then, the others were there.

"Don't damage that fucking creeper!" Kurta said.

But there was no chance of that. The slughead had slid down the wall, limbs still trembling, flukes twisting on his leather jacket like blood guppies dying on a beach.

"Keep back now," Mooney warned the others. "It's birthing itself…"

And it was.

There was a sound like rotten muslin tearing and the flesh-sling sheared open, the creeper sliding free, a wriggling form in a semi-translucent chitinous envelope. It squirmed in there like a worm in a seed, the shell already beginning to crack open from internal pressure as the creeper (the end form of the slug itself) enlarged its mass daily. Now, in order to survive, it would have to emerge. Fetal and dopey and premature, it was vulnerable.

"Don't let it hatch," Kurta said. "West? Hose it down with your extinguisher."

The kid stepped forward and engulfed the shell in white foam. As it bubbled and dissipated, Kurta ordered him to hose it down again. When it evaporated away, the form in the shell was not moving.

"Mooney, bag it," Kurta said.

Mooney was way ahead of him. Using a set of tongs, he gripped the slug shell and dropped it into a red biohazard bag that The Pole held open for him. He dropped a couple of cold packs in with it, squeezing them first to activate the ammonium nitrate. Then he double sealed the bag.

"Outstanding," Kurta told him. "Now get that back to the APC. Go ahead, Speng, you go with him. Don't let anything happen to it."

"Should I call it in?" Spengler asked.

"No. Let's get this place cleaned out first or we'll just have to come back tomorrow."

"Roger that," Spengler said.

"And Speng?" Kurta said.

"Yeah?"

"Nice fucking work."

As Spengler went back with Mooney, he was more than aware of the begrudging tone in Kurta's voice. *Musta just about made him bleed to fucking say that.* He grinned. If he could manage to bag a couple more creepers, the major would give him Kurta's job.

For the first time in a long time, he had something to shoot for.

9

It was the waiting that got under West's skin.

Sure, he was the new guy, the NFG and all that, and his skin wasn't as thick as that of the rest of the slug-hunters, etc., etc. Still, the waiting got to him. The silence wrapped him up and filled his belly with hot tacks. When it got real bad like this, he prayed for contact. He prayed some slughead would jump out at them.

Anything but this.

His heart was pounding and sweat was beading his face. His nerves felt as if they'd been filed to sharp points. He had an image of himself in his head—bug-eyed, lips trembling, knees knocking, and hair standing on end like Moe Howard in an old Columbia short. He figured it wasn't too far from the truth.

"Hang back now," Kurta said over the headset. He was crouched down and he wanted the others to do the same. "Stay put until I give the word. And no shooting. Get your fingers off those triggers right now."

West waited there with The Pole who absolutely fucking hated him. Even in his hot suit, he swore he could feel the bad vibes coming off the man. They had teeth and they wanted to bite him. Had they been truly alone, he figured The Pole would have been riding his shit about now. But Kurta could hear everything they said so The Pole kept his mouth shut.

"Okay," Kurta said. "Get up here."

They jogged forward. Kurta was ahead. They could see his light beam. They closed in on him.

"We've had some action here," he explained.

On the floor, in the beam of his light, were some human remains. They weren't very nice to look at. It was hard to say whether they had belonged to a man or a woman. Whichever it was, they had been split neatly from crotch to throat, skin pulled back from either side of the gaping wound. The abdominal cavity had been emptied, genitals torn away. Everything looked violently stripped, bitten, and chewed. Even the face had been worried to the red skull beneath. A loop of intestine was tossed over a steam pipe, but everything else was gone.

Kurta studied the blood trail in his light.
Smeared red footprints led away into the darkness. The slugheads had gorged themselves.

"Let's see where they lead," Kurta said.

He was totally unmoved by any of it; West found that disturbing. His own stomach was flipping over and over.

They followed Kurta deeper into the shaft, now and again finding a few scraps of flesh, an odd dropped finger or two. Then, just ahead, something moved.

Kurta went after it without hesitation, his riot gun held high. What he found was an old guy with a matted white beard. It was just as dirty and greasy as he was, bits of food caught it in it. There were sticks and leaves in his hair. Kurta put the riot gun barrel right in his face.

It was apparent by that point that he was no slughead.

"Well?" Kurta asked him, his voice artificial-sounding as it came through his breathing filter.

The old guy stood there, scrawny, bent by the years. "Looks like death, all right," he said. "Didn't think it would be the spacemen that got me in the end."

"We're not spacemen," The Pole said.

"You're wearing spacesuits, ain't ya?"

Well, he's got us there, West thought.

Kurta, with his customary lack of patience, explained who and what they were.

"The government? You work for the government? Awww, shit, son, now I know you're telling tales," the old man said, the light gleaming off his oily, wrinkled face, illuminating his teeth which were brown with filth. "Ain't no government no more. Ain't nothing no more. All there is, is spacemen like you and rabbits like me and slugfucks looking for fresh meat." He looked over towards West, squinting to see his face behind the bubble. "That's why they leave me alone, boy. I'm old and stringy and tough."

West smiled.

"Where are they?" The Pole asked. "Where are the slugheads?"

"You'll find 'em if you keep going. I saw two or three back there, that's why I'm getting out. Mercy's dead now, so I'm all alone."

"Mercy?"

"She's back there. You probably saw her. They tore her right open and there wasn't a damn thing I could do about it. Now they're full and fat, kind of lazy, all dopey like they get. That's the time to get out, after they feed."

By then, Kurta had lowered his riot gun.

"We should take him back to the bunker, boss," The Pole said. "The major might want to interrogate him."

"Maybe," Kurta said.

"I ain't going anywhere with you!" the old man said. It was clear he meant it. After all, he was standing up to three well-armed men. "I'm free and you ain't taking my freedom away! *Fuck you! Fuck all of you! You can't tell me what to do or where to go! That ain't how it works now! Slugs evened it all out! Ain't no taxes! Ain't no fucking laws! I ain't got to take shit from jarheads like you!"*

The Pole stepped forward. He wasn't about to take crap like that, not from this old sewer rat. West didn't speak his mind. As far as he was concerned, the old man was right. They had no real authority over him.

"Easy," Kurta said. "Nobody's taking you anywhere. We and about fifty other people live in a reinforced bunker thirty miles from here. We have food, shelter, medical. You want to come, you're welcome. You don't want to, get out of my sight."

"You can't let him go!" The Pole said.

"Why not? We have a job to do and that job isn't babysitting crazy people."

"I ain't crazy!" the old man snarled.

"You better go," West told him.

The old party sneered at them. There were things he wanted to say, but as he pointed out, he wasn't crazy, so he took off down the shaft into the darkness.

The Pole said, "That might be a mistake, letting him go like that."

"Why?" West said. "What possible harm can he do?"

"I wasn't talking to you, you little puppy."

"Oh, kiss my ass, big man."

"Fuck did you say?"

"All right," Kurta said, getting in-between them. "The old man wasn't carrying a slug, so he's not our concern. We gave him the option to come with us, he refused. He's not our problem."

The Pole didn't like it, but he sucked it up because he knew damn well that Kurta didn't give a damn about his opinion. He glared at West through the bubble of his helmet and West glared right back.

Go ahead, West found himself thinking. *Make your move. I've had it right up to here with you.*

"Okay," Kurta said. "Enough. Pole? Take the point." Which The Pole did, begrudgingly.

10

He distanced himself from Kurta and West, getting farther ahead than he usually would have. But he wanted that space. He did not trust the relationship that was developing between them.

The steam tunnel opened into another cellar and he called it in. "I don't think we've been in here before. I'm going in for a look."

"Wait for us," came Kurta's reply. "Don't go in there alone. Repeat: do not go in there alone."

Yeah, bullshit, The Pole thought.

He popped the grating from the tunnel wall and stepped into the cellar. He saw the usual: discarded bedsprings, bikes, heaped cartons, a lot of cast-off junk.

He stepped in further.

He could see some kind of gigantic, antiquated boiler plant that probably predated the steam tunnel system itself. It was a real monstrosity with pipes reaching in every which direction like the tentacles of a deep-sea squid. It had an out-of-place, out-of-time look to it like some colossal, overly complex machine out of a steampunk novel. He figured this is what the reactor of Verne's *Nautilus* must have looked like.

He stepped around it carefully, knowing that Kurta was going to be pissed but not really caring. He had to squeeze between it and a huge pillar-like support beam.

That was when the floor fell away beneath him.

He cried out, sliding on his ass into some chasm beneath the floor of the cellar. He came to rest in standing water. The only thing that was injured was his pride. He pulled himself up, scanning about with his flashlight beam.

What in the hell?

Kurta was on the headset, demanding to know what was going on.

"I fell into a fucking hole," The Pole explained.

"I told you to wait!"

"Yeah, yeah, yeah. Well, I didn't."

Kurta reamed his ass over the headset, but The Pole wasn't even paying attention by that point. His tactical light was showing him standing water, rubble…and bones. Human bones jutting up from the muck and various necrotic remains that were feverish with maggots and flies, the latter filling his flashlight beam in buzzing clouds.

He saw light beams above as Kurta and West arrived.

"Other side of the boiler, watch it," The Pole told them.

"The floor's gone…must have dropped away into this pit."

Kurta grumbled over the headset.

What the hell had happened here? That's what The Pole was wondering. Some kind of subsidence? It was hard to say. These buildings were all old, Victorian relics that should have been torn down years ago. Before the slugs came, this entire area was a slum, a high-crime area full of whores and drug addicts, gangs and crack houses. Jesus, even if they wiped out the slugs, who was going to want to live here?

He heard something just ahead.

Shit.

Gripping his riot gun, he moved around a pile of rubble, the water getting deeper. It had been up to his knees and now it was getting up to his hips. It wouldn't be a good idea to go too far; he might fall into an even deeper pit and drown. There.

More rubble and bones, the well-picked husk of a torso. The water rippled. It splashed.

The Pole sucked in a breath and saw a form rise from the slop. It was a woman…or had been once upon a time…but now she was a crumbling, waterlogged zombie with a face of running mucus, clutching a slug to her belly like a writhing newborn. She must have been in the late stages because she seemed to be undergoing some morbid liquefaction. Her body, as it rose from the water, looked as if it was being engulfed by a jellyfish, a mass of slime and bubbling putrefaction.

The Pole screamed at the sight of her.

It rolled right out of him such was the horror he felt. He fumbled his riot gun, nearly dropping it into the watery slush. The light bobbled, shadows jumping wildly about him.

She opened her mouth and a gushing sludge came pouring out like watery vomit.

The Pole, out of his head at the sight of her, jerked the trigger, racked the pump, jerked it again, repeated this four times until she was a squirming putrescence floating before him.

By then, the flashlight beams of the others were spearing down into the steaming hollow.

Right away, as the woman's blasted carcass sank, her slug emerged in the oily water. It surfaced like a trout seeking a caddisfly. It looped in the water, its fleshy, phallic bulk swimming towards The Pole like a sea snake.

He did not hesitate.

He blasted it to fragments.

"We better get him out of there before more show," West said, and for once, The Pole was in complete agreement with him.

Staring down into the hollow, Kurta said, "Sure…but how are we going to do that?"

The Pole wasn't sure himself.

The walls of the chasm seemed to be made of loose, slimy rubble and what might have been soft clay.

"We'll need rope," West said. "There's some twine back there. I'll get it."

He disappeared, and The Pole found himself staring up at Kurta whose light beam was on him like a spot.

"I told you to wait for us, dipshit," Kurta said.

"I thought I'd have a look."

"Against my orders."

The Pole felt sweaty and small in his hotsuit. "Yeah, my mistake, boss."

"You're starting to make a lot of them." Kurta kept the light on him. "Before the kid gets back, I want you to understand that if you disregard my orders one more fucking time, you're off the team. You'll be clearing corpses in the streets. You got me?"

"Yeah. I got you."

West returned with twine bundled around his arm. "This should be enough. Let me unwind it."

"Fuck it," Kurta said. "I decided to leave him down there."

He stomped away and West watched him go. "I'll get you out, man. Just hang tight."

"I know you will, kid. You're one of the good ones."

As the twine was tossed down to him, his feelings concerning West began to shift. But his feelings concerning Kurta only deepened. *I'll get that fucker. Sooner or later, I'll get that fucker.*

11

Kurta decided they wouldn't bother backtracking into the steam tunnels. After West got The Pole out of the pit, he led them around the chasm, weaving through the dark until he saw a set of stairs leading up.

"Let's call it a day," he said.

He got no arguments on that score. They followed him up a rickety set of stairs to the first floor. The door at the top was open so they didn't have to blast it free.

It was dark up there. Most of the windows were boarded over. The place had been waiting for the wrecking ball long before the slugs wormed their way into existence. He led them down a corridor, came around a bend and heard someone laughing.

Giggling.

It unnerved him the darkness. It wasn't a happy sound, but the low, evil cackling of a mind that was sheared right open, all the good stuff having leaked out and only the blatant psychosis of the human condition left behind.

He told the others to hang back.

He clutched his riot gun, duckwalking forward, his eyes wide, his mouth a pale line behind the helmet bubble. His light beam picked out a shape crouched on the stairs. A man. Even with the light full in its face, blinding in its intensity, the figure could not stop giggling: *"Eh…heh…heh…eh…heh…heh…heh…"*

"What's your damage?" Kurta asked him, but it was obvious by that point. Here was another street person who'd probably been suffering some sort of dementia before the coming of the slugs. Like many of the others, he'd relished his new-found freedom when laws no longer existed and he could do anything he wanted, anytime he wanted. He'd hid out in the city and the slugs had found him.

He was dressed in a natty overcoat that he'd probably swiped off a mannequin in City Centre, wool pants with grubby knees, and hiking boots with black plastic garbage bags duct-taped to them. He clutched his slug with both hands, giggling and rocking back and forth as if it were a baby he was trying to get to sleep. His face was pale, almost gray, eyeballs jutting from purple sockets. He was sweating and shaking, totally stoned on what his slug and its attendant flukes were juicing him with. Early stages for sure. The hunger had not yet set into him which meant the slug was still in the process of hot-wiring his brain.

"I'm going to have to kill you," Kurta said, stepping back and establishing a field of fire. "You understand that, don't you?"

Of course, this guy didn't understand at all.

It was like trying to explain string theory to a hedgehog; dude was just too far gone. And Kurta understood that part. Boy, did he ever. He remembered very well the rapture of the needle. When you had a fix, nothing else mattered. Not a damn thing. The memory of it made his scalp sweat.

It's still got you, he thought. *Even these many years later, it's still got you.*

Not that this was any surprise.

In their sweeps of the city, he'd come across stashes of heroin before. The sight of it always made his palms greasy. If The Pole or any of the others were to discover his past, it wouldn't be good. He could just about imagine how Spengler

47

or The Pole might use it against him. The major might even have reservations if he knew that a junkie was leading Ex-3.

But they're not going to know. I lost my wife, my family, my job, every fucking thing because of the needle. I won't have that happen again.

The slughead looked up as Kurta shouldered his riot gun and pulled out the Colt Python .357. The sluggo was stoned, motor functions impaired. He jerked with spasms, making orgasmic sounds as they rolled through him. He was bovine and stupid. He giggled and licked his lips with a swollen tongue.

"What do you got?" West asked as he approached.

"Newbie," Kurta said.

The Pole laughed at the slughead's predicament. The giggling. The spasms. The way his eyes rolled dreamily in his head. "Must be good shit he's dosed with."

"What happens if you tear that slug off him?" West asked. The Pole laughed dryly. "Nothing good, kid. For one thing, Mr. Host here will not like you doing it. He looks placid enough, don't he? Pissed out of his mind, shitted right out? Sure. Try and rip that slug off…it'll take four guys to hold him down. He'll go absolutely berserk."

The host stared up at the men with that look Kurta had seen when he was a teenager when some good dope was making the rounds. *Hey, man, you wanna a hit? Take a toke and hold your smoke.* Even as they watched, it looked like capillaries were rupturing in his face, purple-blue star blisters forming.

"Eh…heh…heh…eh…heh…heh…heh," went the sluggo, teeth bloodied and eyes going yellow.

Kurta pulled the trigger.

The round cored his left eye socket quite neatly, then kicked out the back of his head. Right away, as he slumped over, his slug began to move. Flukes tumbled from his shattered skull.

"Burn him," Kurta said, stepping way back with West.

The Pole obliged, toasting Mr. Host and his attendant creepy-crawlies.

And that's when all hell broke loose.

12

As three slugheads came shambling out of the darkness, West opened up with his M4, drilling two three-shot bursts into them. He drove them back but momentarily. Suddenly, it seemed like they were everywhere—coming down the stairs, stumbling right over the burning body of the giggling man; filling the corridors, massing, shrieking and hissing, driven by the voracious parasites that rode them, demanding to be filled, to be satisfied.

"WATCH IT!" Kurta called out.

He brought up his riot gun and fired point-blank, splashing the face off one, racking the pump, and giving another two good shots that nearly tore her in half...still, she crawled forward.

West, panicking, emptied his clip into a drooling, growling pack, and the only thing that saved him from being completely overwhelmed was The Pole who lit them up with his flamethrower. Fire gushed from it, enveloping them, and they screeched in agony. Still, crackling and popping, the air pungent with the oily smoke of their cremating hides and burnt hair, they stumbled forward, finally dropping, human slag.

It gave West time to slap another magazine into his M4.

The Pole torched the ones on the stairs and engulfed another crowd coming from the opposite corridor. The flames licked up the walls, furniture and draperies blazing away.

The building was burning by then. He had put out so much fire that no extinguisher in the world could hope to cope with it.

Kurta knew there was only one way out and that was to retreat right through an even dozen slugheads that were between them and the door.

He charged forward, firing round after round, trying to disperse them. West and The Pole followed suit...but soon enough the enemy were among them and it was a deadly hand-to-hand contest.

Kurta blew one slughead away and another leaped at him, swinging something—a chair leg, a broomstick, it was hard to be sure—and it cracked against the side of his helmet, the force of the blow nearly putting him down. He smashed the pistol-grip of his riot gun into a mucid face that seemed to be composed mainly of gray and red pulp.

Its owner, a naked guy whose body was pocked with black ulcers, made a squealing sound and came back for more.

Kurta obliged, sticking the barrel of the riot gun right in his face and blowing his head clean off. Two more jumped out at him, gurgling and screeching. He shot one of them, fired at the other and missed. Then hands were clawing out at him from every direction and the riot gun was plucked from his grip.

A woman grabbed him from behind and two more charged into the fray to finish him off.

The Pole threw off an attacker and blasted one of the sluggos away from Kurta, and as the other leaped forward, Kurta stomped him in the belly with his boot, squishing the spongy mass of his slug in its flesh-sling. That put the slughead right to his knees and Kurta punted him in the head. It was sheer pandemonium.

West went down beneath three women, his M4 lost in the confusion. They straddled him, clawing at the bubble of his helmet, leaving streaks of gore over the Plexiglas.

Kurta, .357 Python in his hand, knocked two sluggos aside, wiped a smear of brain matter from his bubble, and drilled two of the woman with headshots. Their skulls exploded, blood and tissue erupting in bright red fountains. The third came at him, and he gave her a round right in the belly that easily bisected her slug-sling and what it carried. She went down, looking up at him, agonized and deranged, her face a web of rot. He jammed the barrel into her mouth and blew her away.

The Pole kept shooting until his riot gun was empty, then he used it as a club, smashing faces and cracking open skulls. Splashed with blood and smeared with tissue and ribbons of gore, he fought on until a big slughead—a *really, really* big slughead that looked like he'd been an outlaw biker in life— seized him. The sluggo gripped him by the helmet with massive hands to either side, lifting him right off the ground. Maybe it was his intention to pluck the helmet free.

But The Pole did not give in.

He'd been in tighter situations than this (he told himself), so he pulled his knife and went straight for the sluggo's family jewels. In this case, not his nuts but the slug-sheath webbed to his belly. The Pole jabbed the blade of his K-bar right into it again and again.

The slug, a swollen horror that seemed to be nearly the size of his forearm, sheared itself free, cut nearly in half. It coiled and squirmed, spilling brown blood and making a sound like a shrill, whirring motor.

The sluggo still gripped him so The Pole kept stabbing his parasite with the knife.

The effect was instantaneous.

Old Mr. Sluggo let go with a great howling shriek, spraying The Pole's helmet bubble with a bloody mist.

Then he literally came apart at the seams.

Holy oh Jesus H. Christ did he ever.

Somewhere in his dreaming/scheming/zombified mind, there was a memory of a guy named John Q. Schenks who pulled six years hard time at Rahway State Prison for armed robbery and was a patched blood member of the Devil's Disciples motorcycle club.

But that was so much psychobabble mental mulch now because it was BEFORE and not NOW.

Now there was only a nameless servitor with an especially large leech hugging his belly, shooting him up with neuropharmaceuticals and his fluke-infested brain was rioting at terminal velocity.

There was thunder and lightning in his skull, a perpetual drumming BOOM-BADA-BOOM-BADA-BOOM-BOOM-BAM! that made him fly like he'd never flown before. He was a bag about to pop, an adrenaline-juiced carcass stretching like elastic to the breaking point as his gray matter boiled in his skull like hot red slush and thoughts skipped through the chaos, OH YES OH YES OH YES OH MY DEAR CHRIST IT'S BIGGER IT'S BADDER THAN EVER BEFORE!

And like The Who had said, he could see for miles and miles into the narrow fluctuating channel of his psyche and then...then it was too much, overdosed, overloaded, critical mass reached, and his spine was an electric eel writhing inside him, his organs macerating, his neurons imploding, his skin splitting open—

And then...

And then...

And then his face inflated as if it had been stung by a dozen jellyfish into a purple-blue bag of meat and his eyes blew free from their sockets via some weird, immense internal hydrostatic pressure. At the same time they went, blood gushed from his mouth along with sloughed bits of his esophagus and stomach. He hit the floor, three-hundred pounds of squirming red meat that was infested with flukes.

Kurta saw it happen and knew, in his astonishment, that biker boy's slug had emptied its glands into him like a syringe in its death throes, creating a surge of hormones and endorphins that caused the flukes in his brain to react in kind, emptying themselves, flooding his nervous system with a toxic elixir of opiates.

Biker boy got off like he'd never gotten off in his life, the dopamine response in his brain kindling nuclear fission. But as he rode a rising, spiking wave of pleasure/pain, the chemical brew in his brain created a devastating allergic reaction that literally turned his gray matter to sauce and made him expand like a well-filled helium balloon...until he burst.

Letting out a cry, The Pole clawed his way free, actually sinking into the bleeding, livid mass for a moment before he did so.

Kurta blasted away until he was out of shot and then he spun around and...*shit, the kid, the kid, they got the kid!*

West tried to roll himself up like a pillbug as they buried him alive in a sea of thrashing bodies and clawing hands.

Kurta saw the M4 on the floor and dove for it.

He came up shooting, blowing away three of them and blinding a fourth and then he just charged in, swinging the carbine as they came for him.

And the next thing he knew, he was on his ass and there was nothing he could do for the kid because there was nothing he could do for himself.

And it wasn't just those fucking slugheads, but the parasites from the dead ones, too, looking for new vehicles to ride, new hosts to enslave. One of them, a greasy phallic mass, dun-colored and purple-veined, slithered over the glass of his bubble and some screeching voice inside him cried out in hysteria, *a cock, it's a living fucking cock, I'm going to be parasitized by a giant living cock,* and then lights were spearing through the gloom and he heard gunfire, a sustained volume of gunfire.

The sluggos began to drop away, squealing and pissing blood, writhing on the floor like maggots in carrion and a hand helped Kurta up.

There was Mooney and Spengler.

Fucking heroes.

They'd come to save the day.

Spengler got West and Kurta out of there as The Pole and Mooney opened up with their flame-throwers and set a four-alarm fire burning, a weenie roast of epic proportions.

By the time they made it out into the street, the whole goddamn building was going up, fire licking out of the windows and a funnel of churning black smoke pouring out of the doorway.

When they were back at the APC, all Kurta could say was, "Thanks, I won't forget it."

Mooney shrugged. "Hey, that's what we're here for."

But Spengler, smiling a cocky grin, knowing he had not only nabbed himself an unborn creeper but had rescued the team leader and the boy wonder from certain parasitization— *showing uncommon valor against an overwhelming opposing force*—planned on holding him to that.

13

Six hours after Ex-3 came back in and were given their chemical showers, debriefing, and turned their creeper into the lab boys, the second-floor meeting room at the bunker was party central.

The classic rock was cranking and the booze was flowing.

Time to kick back, drink some beer, smoke some bud, and let the world go away. Spengler was a hero and he was having a hero's sort of party. A bottle of Jack Daniels in one hand and an ex-stripper named Daniella Creed in the other, he was regaling everyone with randy tales of hunting slugheads. Putting them down so they didn't get back up, smashing loose slugs under his boots, and toasting them with his flamethrower. The war was winnable, he told anyone within earshot, and they were winning it day by day.

Kurta didn't bother commenting on that.

He'd been running Ex-3 for fourteen months and had gone through no less than sixteen exterminators in that time. Still, though, people were always ready to join up. They didn't get truly disillusioned until they got into the thick of things. If they lasted long enough, they learned to keep their traps shut like Kurta or became increasingly cynical like The Pole. But tonight? Hell, victory was at hand.

If you didn't believe that, all you had to do was listen to Spengler and his proclamations of a slug-free world.

He was a first-class hero and he was living it up, milking it for everything it was worth. Major Trucks was impressed by how Mooney and he had pulled Kurta's ass out of the flames, not to mention the creeper that Dr. Dewarvis and the other labcoat johnnies had swiftly secreted down in the lab. Dewarvis was ecstatic and that made the major happy and when he was happy, the booze came out and anyone not on duty was welcome to drink themselves silly as long as they didn't cause any trouble.

Those who had girlfriends were either dancing or drunkenly necking or had slipped back to their private quarters to slap skin. Those who didn't, just stood around and fantasized about everyone else's girlfriends, drinking away their frustrations or getting mean and pissy like The Pole. He'd already been in three fights that Kurta broke up and a fourth was in the offing because the other teams were there—Ex-1 and 2, 3 and 7, elements of 5. Ex-4 was the ready reaction team in case the shit hit the fan and perimeter security had to be beefed up, as in the case of an all-out assault by a slughead force. So they were not invited. Each team was competitive with the others, claiming a higher body count and more neighborhoods cleared. Something which was getting on The Pole's nerves.

"Tell us about it again, baby," Daniella said to Spengler in her honey-sweet Alabama purr.

Which Spengler did, of course.

Daniella was a tall redhead with a blue ribbon set of tatas (as The Pole had pointed out more than once) who tended to attach herself to whatever man was receiving the most kudos. She was pretty, but there was something cruel and cunning in her face that some just did not like.

It was a given that Spengler would be screwing her tonight because that's how she worked.

There was an attractive, perky blonde named Lisa Hilsson who was dancing with West. He was young, sweet-natured, and good-looking. She made the perfect counterpart to him. Something which made more than one man jealous. She was a nurse and a damn good one, people said. Kurta had had a brief relationship with her until one night, drunk out of his mind, he told her that the slug infestation was exactly what the human race deserved. Lisa, who had a daughter with her in the bunker, did not want to hear such things.

Thinking back on that, Kurta laughed. Because it was always easier to laugh than cry.

He watched the roosters strutting about and the hens shaking their tail feathers and thought, *I'm seeing the end of a way of life. Another year tops and there won't be parties like this anymore. In fact, there fucking won't be anything.* He sipped his drink, pulled off a cigarette, and listened to The Pole who was about ten feet away, getting louder by the moment.

"That's the thing," he said, a certain species of contempt in his voice. "See, when the wigglers come out of their eggs, they can attach them-fucking-selves to anything. I've seen it. They can get in your hair, under your collar, in your shoes. They can ride on you for days before they sucker themselves to your belly."

"That's why we get decontaminated," Philly from Ex-5 informed him. "That's why we take chemical baths."

"Oh really, big kahuna? How do you think those two bunkers got in-fucking-fested over at Wright-Patterson? How do you think our military fell one base at a time? How do you think we're in a sorry, rag-fucking-tag situation like this waiting for the end?"

The more The Pole drank, the more he began to insert *fuck* into any word he could.

Philly said, "Oh, here we go. Doom and gloom. I was waiting for it."

"Maybe there wouldn't be so much doom and fucking gloom if you ass-fucking-holes with Five were doing your jobs."

"What the hell you mean by that?"

"I mean what I fucking say," The Pole said. "Three pulls the shit week after week while you puppies are busy sucking each other's dicks. It's em-fucking-barrassing."

"Maybe you better watch your mouth," Philly said.

"And maybe you should suck my dick, Mr. Ex-fucking-terminator and gargle with my fucking cum—"

Bang.

Philly hit him. Straight jab, it put The Pole to his knees but it didn't keep him there. He came up swinging, catching Philly with a roundhouse shot before Philly drilled him again. As The Pole came back for more, Philly made a grab for him but was brushed aside by a big dude they called Downtown. He held the combatants apart at arm's length. He jabbed a finger at The Pole's chest. "Maybe you better settle down."

"And maybe your mother should have kept her legs crossed."

That's all it took.

Downtown hit The Pole and The Pole hit Philly and Spengler dove on Downtown. Pretty soon, Three and Five were going at it. Kurta charged in, took a couple shots, kneed Downtown in the nuts and dropped Philly. "ENOUGH!" he said. "ENOUGH OF THIS SHIT OR THE FUCKING PARTY'S OVER!"

Everyone pulled back, not wanting to piss Kurta off because he had the major's ear. That and the fact that he was the most successful exterminator in the bunker and the others routinely tried to get on his team.

The party resumed, but the good cheer was gone. Three and Five eyed each other warily, keeping on opposite sides of the room. Janis D, the team leader of Five, apologized to Kurta, but Kurta told her it was his man who had started it. Every time there was bullshit in the offing, you could almost be sure The Pole was involved.

It was getting old.

The Pole, bruised and bloodied but refusing medical aid, staggered over and bumped into Kurta. "Thanks for standing up for me, my brother," he said.

"Oh, shut the fuck up," Kurta told him.

He went and sat in the corner, nursing a beer that tasted skunky and warm, dragging off a cigarette that didn't taste much better. *Yeah, it's all getting old,* he thought, *and it's been that way for a long time now. And there ain't no way out.* And there wasn't, not really. Even if you wanted to get away from it, strike out on your own…where would you go? There were no slug-free zones in the world that he'd ever heard of. This was it. This was all there was.

West came over with Lisa Hilsson. She smiled at Kurta and he blew her off. He was glad, secretly, that she was with West. They made a nice couple. But for all that, he couldn't pretend that he was happy she'd dumped him. It still hurt. So he masked it with callous indifference.

When she went off to get a drink, West, who was pretty fucked up, said, "Sometimes I'm glad it's like this. I just wasn't making it the way things were before, you know? I just couldn't find my place. I went through one job after the other. So maybe it's better things are like this. Maybe it's better for me."

Kurta didn't respond. He blinked, sipped his beer, and dragged off his cigarette.

West thought about what he'd just said, a crazy look in his eyes. "No, that's bullshit. I don't think that way at all. I don't even know why I said it."

"People say things they don't mean all the time," Kurta told him.

West nodded. "I guess…I guess if it has to be this way, I'm glad I'm with you. With Three. It's the best I can hope for."

Kurta didn't comment on that either because it was bullshit, only he didn't want to ruin the kid's drunken fantasy by telling him so. Guys on the teams got like that. They'd start drinking and things would just pour out of them. They were looking for a safe zone in their own minds where they could justify what they were doing and make themselves believe that things would be okay in the end. Soldiers probably got like that in every conflict, he supposed. Justifying things to themselves and making themselves believe that what they were doing really mattered even when they knew it didn't.

When West staggered off to the head, Lisa said, "Should I break the uncomfortable silence or will you?"

Kurta smiled. It felt strange; he didn't do it much anymore. "I'm glad you hooked up with West. He's a good kid. You guys can be good together."

"I think so," she said. Then: "There was a time when I thought we'd be good together."

"Then you dumped me."

"I dumped you because you've got a lot of ugliness inside you. I couldn't live with that day after day. You're a cynical asshole, Kurta, and we both know it."

He chuckled sourly. "Do what I fucking do day in and day out and that's how it gets." He lit another cigarette and pulled off it. "Look around you, Lisa. Tell me what you see."

She knew what was coming, but she refused to be baited. "I see people having a good time. I see people blowing off steam. That's what I see."

"You know what I see?" he asked her.

She sighed. "No, but you're going to tell me."

"Yes, I am. I see a bunch of fools who are pretending that there's going to be a next week or a next month or a next year. I see fucking idiots fiddling while Rome burns."

"Same old Kurta."

"Yeah, the song never changes."

"I better go see to West."

"Yeah, you better. Enjoy him. One of these days, I'll be bagging him and he won't be coming home."

She scowled at him, but didn't bother pointing out the obvious: that inside, deep inside, he was festering.

14

After a couple hours of it, Kurta decided he'd had enough. He went to see the major, knowing he was expected. Major Trucks was on the third level and very few ever got to see him. Kurta found him in his office.

"OUTSTANDING WORK TODAY!" he said with his usual volume, something he was incapable of toning down. "SPENGLER REALLY SHOWED HIS STUFF, EH? A CREEPER! THEN HIS RESCUE OF YOU AND WEST! THAT'S THE KIND OF SHIT I LIKE TO SEE!"

"Mooney was in on it, too, sir," Kurta pointed out.

"OF COURSE HE WAS!"

Major Trucks paced back and forth like a good little commander with too much on his plate. He mumbled things to himself, then he turned and looked at Kurta. "I BEEN THINKING!"

"Have you?"

The major ignored the sarcasm. "SPENGLER'S WORKING OUT PRETTY GOOD! WHAT DO YOU THINK ABOUT BUMPING HIM UP TO SECOND-IN-COMMAND OF THREE?"

"I'd say no. He's not up to it," Kurta explained. "And even if he was, that would mean demoting Mooney. We can't do that. Besides, it would mean giving him more rank than The Pole, than Skowalski, and that wouldn't fly. Skowalski's been at it longer."

"I DON'T GIVE A SHIT ABOUT POLITICS! MOONEY AND SKOWALSKI WILL JUST HAVE TO LIVE WITH IT!"

"It's not that simple, sir. You disrupt the pecking order and I'm going to have trouble keeping the team together," Kurta told him. "It's hard enough now."

"WHAT IF I TOLD YOU I ALREADY MADE MY DECISION?"

"Then I'd have to question it."

"WHO THE HELL DO YOU THINK YOU ARE TO QUESTION ME?" the major fumed, droplets of spit spraying into the air. "I MAKE THE FUCKING DECISIONS, NOT YOU! BESIDES, SPENGLER DESERVES THIS! DON'T FORGET THAT HIS OLD MAN WAS A HIGHLY DECORATED MARINE! HE WAS A FUCKING COLONEL IN THE CORPS FOR GODSAKE!"

Kurta refused to budge. "I thought you didn't give a shit about politics?"

"WATCH YOUR FUCKING MOUTH, KURTA! I'M WARNING YOU! YOU PISS ME OFF AND I'LL GIVE THREE TO SPENGLER!"

Kurta stood up. "Why don't you do that…*sir*. Because that idiot'll get them all killed within a single afternoon."
With that, he walked to the door.

"I DIDN'T FUCKING DISMISS YOU!" Major Trucks raged.

"Who gives a shit?" Kurta said. "What're you gonna do? Make me go kill slugs?"

15

There were no secrets in the bunker and all walls have ears as it had been pointed out again and again. Soon enough, the altercation between the major and Kurta filtered back to the party and it wasn't long before Spengler heard about it. The more he drank, the more important he felt.

"It's too bad," he said to Daniella, "but I fucking saw it coming. Kurta's a loose cannon. There was a time when he was really something, but sadly, that time has now passed."

Truth was, of course, that he hated Kurta. Particularly after that thing with Stiv; Kurta just wouldn't let him forget about that business. But now that it appeared he was rising to the top of Three like a turd surfacing in a toilet bowl, he was a big enough man to feel sorry for poor Kurta and his misguided ways.

"What you ought to do," Daniella suggested, "is to go see the major and lay it out for him. I bet he gives you Three before you leave."

"You think so?"

"Oh, I know it! I can feel it."

She laid on the sugar and pressed her breasts up against him, letting him know in no uncertain terms that there was a place in her bed for a man like him. As he swallowed the drinks, she whispered in his ear that she'd always fantasized about getting down on her knees for him.

That was it.

That's all it took (that and a lot of liquor).

Steeling himself, Spengler went below and knocked on the major's door.

"SPENGLER? WHAT THE HELL ARE YOU DOING DOWN HERE?" the major inquired. "WHY AREN'T YOU ENJOYING YOUR PARTY?"

"The party's great, sir," Spengler said, trying to appear confident but not overly so. "But I want to talk to you about things."

"WHAT THINGS?"

"The team, sir. Three. I'm worried about it."

"ARE YOU?"

Spengler nodded. "I have a lot of respect for Kurta, but, honestly, sir, he's really been dropping the ball lately. If I hadn't gotten him out of that mess today, sir, well, he'd no longer be with us. That's the sad truth of the matter. I'm worried his recklessness is going to get us all killed."

"I SEE!" The major contemplated it. "WHAT DO YOU HAVE IN MIND?"

"Sir, though it pains me to say this, I just don't think Kurta's up to it anymore. I'd like you to consider replacing him. At least temporarily."

"WITH WHO?"

"Me, sir. I've been with the team a long time. I know how things work and how they *should* work. My old man was a leader, sir, and it's in my blood to lead. I'm the one you need leading Three, sir."

Major Trucks thought it over. "INTERESTING, INTERESTING! LET ME THINK ON IT A SECOND!"

This was it, this is what Spengler had been waiting for for some time. He could practically feel Daniella's pink, wet mouth sliding up and down on his dick. Wait until Kurta got a load of this. *He deserves it, that's all. He's not fit to lead, not like me.* Spengler watched the major pace back and forth. It was practically a done deal.

Major Trucks got in close, probably to congratulate his new team leader. Spengler beamed.

"I'VE COME TO A DECISION," he announced with his usual volume.

"Yes?" Spengler said.

The major nodded. "I DECIDED THAT I DON'T GIVE ONE HAIRY SHIT WHO YOUR OLD MAN WAS! HE WAS JUST ANOTHER DUMBFUCK JARHEAD! KURTA'S IN CHARGE! DO WHAT HE SAYS, YOU SILLY FUCK, OR I'LL HAVE YOU SHOVELING SHIT AND SUCKING SLUG-SLIME! NOW GET YOUR PISSING FACE OUT OF MY SIGHT! YOU MAKE ME SICK TO MY MOTHERFUCKING STOMACH!"

So that's how Spengler's promotion went.

It was some time before he could work up the nerve to return to the party. By the time he got there, of course, everyone knew what had happened. Daniella had lost interest in him and was actively courting three guys from Five. To make matters worse, everyone was ignoring Spengler...though he did hear a few people giggling behind his back. Apparently, the major had broadcast the entire exchange over the intercom.

All in all, the party was over and the sun had set on his ambitions. There was nothing left to do but get totally shit-faced with The Pole and plot Kurta's overthrow as they did almost nightly.

16

Kurta was glad to be out on the streets with Ex-3 again. Whenever the shit got heavy, he always wanted to be at the bunker, kicking back with a beer in his hand. But after a couple days in that fucking bughouse with that self-deluded, self-indulgent bunch of wingnuts, he was more than ready to get on a one-to-one basis with the slugheads again. At least their behavior was understandable. They weren't a bunch of idiots who traipsed about in a fairy tale la-la land where everything was bunnies and rainbows, avoiding the very real possibility that they were an endangered species poised on the edge of extinction.

He understood now why soldiers coming back from foreign wars could not relate to society in general. After seeing the true nature of darkness and wading through the bleak swamp of the human condition, how could you go back to infantile, mindless, escapist nonsense like backyard barbecues and the NBA, celebrity bullshit and which corporate knob politicians were sucking, Sundays in church and the latest franchise crapfest spawned by Hollywood?

After exterminating sluggos day after day and nearly getting exterminated himself again and again, the people of the bunker made no sense to him.

They were a bunch of scurrying rats in a trap, feigning compassion and unity while their real objectives were filling their bellies and getting their rocks off. But that, he supposed, was the human race laid bare: *gimme, gimme, gimme, fuck you, I got mine.*

Off-Peak Day Single

D

Date of travel
03-APR-24

Valid for one journey

from Edinburgh

to Dunbar

Not valid via Newcastle

See restrictions nre.co.uk/C2
Adult Standard Class
with Two Together Railcard
Refundable and exchangeable for a fee

£5.00X

62593-4043-9541-30-05-00

1402 070424

My InterRail

Explore Europe by train with an Interrail pass.
Go to **myinterrail.co.uk** for details.

Endorsements:

Case in point, where they were now headed: the Southgate Mall. Once a gluttonous enclave of mass consumerism and now a seething nest of slugheads. He wondered sourly what the difference was. Regardless, this was going to be a good one. He felt it right down into his bones.

Pulling off his cigarette, he said, "Okay, you know the scoop. We got a Class-A nest here and the major wants it cleaned out."

That got a few grunts from Ex-3 and more than a few obscenities from The Pole as he drove the APC into the massive parking lot of the mall.

"We're going in through the west entrance," Kurta said. "Ex-Two will take the north and Ex-Five the east. We all have light bands on our helmets. If you see a light band, do not fucking shoot at it. I'll be in contact with the team leaders of Two and Five at all times, coordinating our efforts…but in case we come into contact with each other, don't pull triggers until you know what you're shooting at."

He was expecting some smart-assed comment on that, but he got nothing. Nobody was saying much today. Especially Spengler. Everyone knew what he had done last night—the intercom broadcast left nothing to the imagination. He was keeping pretty quiet about it all. He refused to meet Kurta's eyes, something Kurta found more than a little amusing.

Tried to shoot me in the back and shot yourself in the foot, eh?

No matter. Kurta had seen it coming. After Spengler bagged the creeper and rescued them from the slugheads, his ego got so big that his head would barely fit into the APC. Kurta wasn't angry about any of it; he expected nothing less. For Spengler to do anything else would have been going against character.

And Kurta didn't want that.

He liked his boys to be predictable and good old Speng was certainly that.

The Pole stopped the APC just outside the west side entrance. Kurta told everyone to get their helmets on. They checked each other's suits for containment breaches or fatigued material. Everything was a go. Kurta made one last check of everyone's equipment as he always did.

"This is going to be a bad one, isn't it?" West said.

"Let's just say I'm expecting rain," Kurta told him, "and chances are, we're going to get wet."

"I like that," The Pole said.

Mooney gave Kurta the thumbs up and Spengler just brooded. Behind the glass bubble, his face was blank, unreadable.

"You got something on your mind?" Kurta asked him.

The question made the others stop what they were doing because this could be good; this could be high drama and they weren't going to miss out on it.

"No," Spengler said. "Nothing."

The Pole started laughing. "Ah, go ahead, Speng, tell him what's on your mind. Tell him what you really think about him. Don't hold back like last night."

"That's enough," Mooney said.

"Ain't nothing on my mind," Spengler said.

Kurta didn't comment on that. He didn't like Spengler acting withdrawn like this. He was hardly his favorite person in the world, but to see him beaten down and lifeless like this was just no good.

"Whatever's on your mind, Speng, stow it until later."

Spengler nodded. It was obvious he didn't give a shit about anything. He was depressed.

Yeah, Kurta thought, *well boo-fucking-hoo. Welcome to the club, shit-fer-brains.*

He got on the headset and called out to Ex-2 and Ex-5 that they were preparing to engage via the western entrance. He got a "roger" on that.

The ramp dropped on the APC and Kurta led them out. The doors were open beneath the massive KOHL'S sign, so in they went. It looked like a bomb had gone off in there. Merchandise was scattered everywhere, the aisles a tangled mess of shattered glass display cases, dismembered mannequins, clothes and shoes and household wares. It looked like an angry mob had been looking for something and, not finding it, decided to destroy the place.

As Kurta moved forward in the dimness, he noticed that a lot of the clothing was not only very dusty but shredded. Rats and mice must have been having a field day. Immense cobwebs were spun from dangling sale banners overhead to the tops of shelves and racks. He saw rodent droppings scattered about and what he was certain was more than one pile of human excrement.

According to the major, there had been some sort of commune hiding out in the mall, taking advantage of not only the shelter but the abundance of everything from clothes and boots to hardware and sporting goods. They'd been in the mall for months before the slugs showed up, probably brought into their insular little community by an outsider. Once established, the slugs infested as they were wont to do.

Now, this was sluggo central.

Kurta didn't doubt it.

He could almost feel them here waiting. Yes, the rain was definitely going to fall today.

"Get ready," he said over the headset. "I think we're about to step in it."

17

Kurta was the one that heard it—a low, busy slurping punctuated by an occasional crunching sort of noise. It was an awful thing to hear there in the even deadness of that huge store. The noise went on and on. He was reminded of a hound chewing on a meaty steak bone.

"Hang back," he told the others over the headset. "Let me get a look at this before we get caught in it."

By then, of course, they were all hearing it and they had no problem following his order. He stalked forward, sweat beading his brow. He felt afraid and anxious. First contact was always like that. Better to initiate and get it over with than to exist in a perpetual state of anxiety, fearing the unknown.

He was in Housewares.

Dirty, cobwebbed displays of Rachel Ray cookware and Calphalon pots and pans. Shelves of plates and flatware. Islands of Waterford crystal. A chic working kitchen for demonstrations. Relics of a culture long dead now. All of it flaked with dust and spider dirt.

Kurta moved forward, circling around the kitchen, debris crunching under his boots. He paused. Waited. The slurping sound continued unabated. He cut down aisles of small appliances—electric fry pans, blenders, food processors, and roasters—until he was practically on top of the sounds.

Swallowing, he stepped around a service counter and put the tactical light of his Ithaca pump on a shape that squatted at the foot of a Kohl's charge card display. A sexy woman held up a credit card in her long, lovely fingers…something in direct contrast to the slughead at her feet.

What the light showed him was a naked, middle-aged woman with narrow, pendulous breasts and stringy gray hair hanging in her face. Her sallow skin was baggy like an old sack, set with purple sores and glaring black contusions. With her left arm, she cradled the distended slug-sling at her belly which was livid and engorged. It glistened with foul drainage, pulsating like a breathing lung. The slug inside it must have been enormous, maybe not a fully-molted creeper yet but damn close. She cradled it lovingly, rocking it like a fussy infant.

Kurta had seen such obscene motherly devotion in slugheads before, particularly women, as if the parasitization had activated some latent maternal instinct.

Regardless, it was sickening.

But what she was doing was even worse. Set before her was a heap of dead rats she'd apparently collected up. All of them were twisted and broken. He almost felt sorry for them. As he watched, revolted yet curious, she picked up one by the tail with her free hand, bit into its lower belly, then—drawing it savagely down—literally unzipped it with a wet, tearing sound. Then, grunting like a rooting hog, she pressed her face into the aperture and proceeded to suck the rat's entrails and organs free.

It was disgusting.

In fact, *disgusting* didn't even cut it. This was brutally fucking appalling.

She sucked the guts out of it with a sound not unlike someone slurping up Jell-O shots. Then, her corrugated, graying face wet with dripping gore, she chewed away at the carcass, snapping bones in her teeth. Then she tossed the rat into a death pile of others that had been similarly emptied.

As she reached for another, still oblivious to the light in her face, Kurta (who couldn't bear to watch her eat another rat), said through his helmet's external speaker, "Psssst…sluggo…over here…"

Her head snapped in his direction instantly.

Her face twisted into a blood-spattered fright mask, glazed eyes luminous with hate, lips peeled back from bared, crusty teeth. She rose uneasily to her feet, never letting go of her beloved slug. Making a growling sound, she charged.

She made it maybe four feet before the Ithaca in Kurta's hands barked and her head exploded in an eruption of meat, gray matter, and bone splinters.

She hit the floor with a splatting sound.

Kurta flipped her over with his boot.

Her slug-sack was trembling, flexing like the belly of a pregnant woman whose fetus had just rolled over. The slug was working its way free. It didn't take them long to realize the party was over.

And this was going to be a big one.

A real monster.

"Hell's going on, Kurt?" Mooney said over the headset. "You in one piece over there?"

"Yeah, but a sluggie isn't. You boys might as well join me. You'll find me in Housewares."

18

When they finally arrived, the slug had just made its appearance. It sheared a hole in the sack and pushed itself free like a graveworm from a dead man's eye socket. It was over a foot in length, a worming muscular mass that bulged as it inched forward. It was a washed-out gray-blue, corded with arteries thick as malted straws.

"Want me to toast it?" The Pole asked.

"It's a big one," West said. "Doc Dewarvis said he wants the big ones."

"I got a big one for him," The Pole said.

Mooney laughed.

Kurta just shook his head. "Fuck him. You got any idea how many specimens I've brought in for that asshole? Gotta be two dozen slugs, four or five creepers, jars of fucking wigglers, and half a dozen specimen bags full of eggs. What has he done with them? *Nothing.* More exhibits for his fucked up zoo down in Bio."

Mooney laughed again. "You remember that time he wanted a brain?"

Kurta remembered all right.

He listened while Mooney told the story. Dewarvis wanted to study the chemical transmission from flukes into a host's brain, so Kurta cut the brain out of the skull of a freshly-killed sluggo...complete with the flukes that infested it.

"What does he do with all that nasty shit?" West asked.

"Nobody knows for sure," The Pole said. "Bio is off limits to everyone but the doc, his techs, and the major. I heard he's got shit that would turn your stomach. Human guinea pigs, you name it."

"Shit, I'd like to see that."

"No way. It's biohazard level four, kid. Nobody gets in there," Mooney explained. "And if they do, they don't get out again."

Kurta had heard it all before. Maybe it was bullshit, but then, maybe not. He stepped back a few feet as the slug started to crawl in his direction. "Well," he said, "Doc ain't getting this one. Unless you want to bag it for him, Speng."

Spengler just said, "No, never again."

Why did you do that? Kurta asked himself. *Guy's already down, do you gotta keep kicking him?*

The truth was, he didn't know why he said it. He just didn't know. Maybe it was like Lisa Hilsson had said, he was a miserable, pessimistic piece of shit who wasn't happy unless he brought everyone down to his level.

The slug was getting closer. It spat a gob of psychotropic goo at Kurta and missed. It wanted a new mother in the worst possible way, but it wasn't going to get one. He racked the pump on the Ithaca and blew it into slimy fragments.

The Pole sighed. "Too bad. It was such a pretty one, too."

19

After Kohl's, they got out into the mall proper and they could hear the gunfire of Ex-2 and Ex-5 making contact, the former on the other end of the mall down towards J.C. Penney and the latter upstairs. Kurta was on the com with them and it was getting hot and heavy, but Janis D and Pennworthy (the team leaders of Ex-5 and Ex-2, respectively), were not requesting backup.

Not just yet.

Kurta led the others forward, past Sephora, Hot Topic, and Starbucks. The corridor was a mess, trashcans tipped over, benches covered with bird shit, filth and debris and loose garbage everywhere. Plate glass windows were shattered or streaked with grime. There was a fountain at the end which, of course, had long since ceased to run. In the tepid, green-slimed water, the remains of two or three bloated white corpses bobbed, flies rising from them like clouds of soot. There were a couple of skeletons sunken to the bottom. They looked like they belonged to children. Pigeons cooed from their new digs in Old Navy. Weeds had actually sprouted from cracks in the floor, fed by the sunlight streaming in from the skylights high above where swifts and rooks dipped and circled.

It was insane, perfectly insane.

Kurta had been there many times back in the day when it was still a functioning entity. He knew if they walked on for a time, the corridor would split off to Sears on one side and the food court on the other, which was a massive, airy space meant to resemble a town square with its little shops, statuary, flowers and plants growing everywhere. He thought of Sbarro and Orange Julius, Dairy Queen and Nathan's Famous Hot Dogs and Baskin-Robbins…all that junk food he'd loved and would never, ever taste again.

There was something more than a little sad about that.

"Shouldn't we be checking out these shops?" West asked. "Clearing them out?"

Kurta stopped and looked at him. "Those places are dark rat holes, kid. You want to charge in there, tripping over merchandise, squeezing in-between the aisles with slugheads jumping out at you?"

"Guess not."

"Trust me, if they're here, they'll come for us. They won't be able to help themselves."

"I say we let the kid go in by himself," The Pole said. "Use him as bait. Then when he comes running out with thirty of 'em on his ass, we'll fucking toast 'em."

"Fuck that," West said.

The Pole laughed. "Come on, kid. Think of my entertainment here."

"Let's do it my way," Kurta said.

And his way worked, because not five minutes later, they got some action.

20

It came from Build-a-Bear Workshop of all places.

Six or seven of them charged, drooling and hissing, eyes like glimmering silver coins. They were driven forward by the voracious appetites of their slugs which had already drained them down to walking skeletons.

"PUT 'EM DOWN!" Kurta cried out.

Nobody hesitated. M4 carbines and Ithaca riot guns began firing and it was a real turkey shoot.

The slugheads charged forward and rounds ripped through them, pulverizing them, spraying their anatomy in every direction.

Then The Pole stepped forward and turned his flamethrower on them. Even torn apart as they were, they jumped and jerked as the flames overwhelmed them. A minute later, it was done with—they were carbonized wraiths, snapping and popping, breaking apart.

It was at times like this that Kurta was glad for the filters on the helmets because the stench must have been unbelievable.

"Something moved in there. I saw it," West said.

All eyes turned to Build-a-Bear. Yes, now they saw it, too, a sort of slinking shape pulling away from the light. West volunteered to go in, but The Pole brushed him aside.

"Let me show you how this is done," he said.

Kurta let him go. The Pole might have been a lot of things, but cowardly certainly wasn't one of them. He was a good killer who never pulled any John Wayne hero fantasy shit.

His own survival was always paramount in his mind.

While the others hung back, he stepped away from the roasting slughead corpses and stepped into Build-a-Bear. Right away, the sluggo hissed. The Pole put his light on him and hosed him down with the flamethrower…then he retreated.

The slughead, blazing bright and throwing off greasy plumes of black smoke, went wild in his last moments. He spun, he whirled, he smashed into the shelves that held all the little costumes for the stuffed animals, lighting them up. He finally tripped and stumbled into a wall of display bears and they started to burn, too. Within seconds, it seemed, the entire shop was going up, the fire spreading in every direction.

"I always fucking hated Teddy Bears," The Pole said.

"The sterilization has begun," Mooney said.

And then, suddenly, there were slugheads everywhere. They poured out of Bath & Body, Hot Topic, and Footlocker. Waves of them converging, it seemed, from every possible direction, filling the corridor in an army of slavering, deranged demons bent on one mission in their miserable existences: exterminating the men who had come to exterminate them.

"PULL BACK!" Kurta cried over the headset. "PULL THE FUCK BACK!"

It was the only logical choice of action.

They pulled back towards the dead escalators, noticing with more than a little unease that there were sluggos on the upper floor staring down at them. They hadn't started coming down the escalator yet, but they would. It was only a matter of time.

Meanwhile, the horde charged in for the kill.

Ex-3 formed ranks and started pouring everything they had at them—the M4s, the Ithacas, tossing a few grenades to thin the ranks. But it was never quite enough. For every one put down, there were three or four others coming in for the kill. Blasted, perforated, burning, and pitted with shrapnel, they still kept coming. And Ex-3 could only hope to fight this sort of rearguard action for so long.

Kurta ordered Mooney and The Pole forward with the flamethrowers, and they put out a wall of fire that turned most of the slugheads back. Some of them, absolutely berserk with fury, rushed forward right into the flames, screaming as they were engulfed. A few more motivated individuals actually made it through the cordon of fire to collapse at the feet of Ex-3 as charred husks.

The flames giving them a momentary margin of safety, Kurta called Pennworthy with Ex-2 and Janis D with Ex-5. Both teams were in the shit, sluggos converging from every direction. What had started as a mop-up operation had now become a battle for survival.

"We're getting the fuck out," Janis D said. "There's too many! I already lost one and I got another injured! We're making for the APC…if we can reach it!"

Pennworthy said the same thing. He was down to three including himself. There was no way they could handle the numbers they were seeing.

Which pretty much made up Kurta's mind.

West and Mooney were all for it, but Spengler started laughing when he heard it. "Ha! Not the great fucking Kurta pussying out on us? I never thought I'd live to see the day."

"That'll do," Kurta told him.

And The Pole said, "I don't know, Kurt. You always tell us to speak our minds. Speng is just speaking his mind."

"Yeah," Spengler said. "That's all I'm doing."

Kurta, feeling his blood boiling under his skin, said, "No, Speng, that's not what you're doing. You've been brooding

ever since the major spanked you and we all know it. I was
going to give you a pass on this. I wasn't going to embarrass
you by mentioning how you went to see Trucks, licking his
balls to get my job. I wasn't going to bring up the fact that
you stabbed me in the fucking back. I was going to let it go.
But since you don't want that, let me tell you this, you
pathetic little twat. This is your last op with us. You're a
fucking liability. Come Monday, you'll be cleaning up
bodies in the street or mopping out shitters or baking fucking
cookies for the kids in the galley—but you won't be here.
You won't be doing a man's job with other men because you
don't have the nuts for it."

Spengler leaped.

It was an automatic response. He did not even think about
it. Kurta had publicly emasculated him and there had to be
payback for that. So, as the flames licked around them, the
slughead corpses hissing and crackling, black smoke filling
the air in a sickening pall, Spengler launched himself at
Kurta.

But Kurta was no dummy.

He knew Spengler. Spengler was simple-minded, strictly a
push-button type. You pressed button A, he got pissed off.
You pressed button B, he took a swing at you. He was too
stupid to mount a successful verbal counterattack so he did
what came naturally to macho sock puppets without brains:
he came in for the kill.

Kurta baited him, and when he came, he rammed him in
the face bubble with the pistol grip of his Ithaca. Spengler
went down hard. His bubble was visibly scratched.

"YOU FUCKING CRACKED IT!" he wailed. "YOU
FUCKING CRACKED MY BUBBLE!"

"It's a scratch," Mooney told him, knowing as they all did
that the Acrylite bubbles had the same tensile strength as the

canopies of jet fighters. Not much less than a bullet was going crack it.

Spengler climbed to his feet. "YOU MOTHERFUCKER! I'LL FUCKING KILL YOU! I'LL BE CONTAMINATED NOW!"

"Settle down, man," The Pole said, but Spengler knocked him aside.

"FUCK YOU!" he cried. "FUCK ALL OF YOU!"

And then he ran off. Kurta called for him to come back, but it was pointless. Spengler had been at the breaking point for some time and now he was completely out of his head.

"Nice going," The Pole grumbled.

"Stop it," Mooney said.

"No, no," Kurta told him. "Let him hang himself. Because what I said to Spengler goes for him, too. It's his last day with Three."

Maybe The Pole would have backed off or argued his case, but there was no time because the slugheads were mounting another assault, this one more stealthy. As the drama of Ex-3 played out, they were creeping in from every quarter. When West pointed that out, Kurta saw them, their dark shapes filling the corridor.

Right then, he knew they were in deeper shit than they could have imagined.

21

"WATCH IT! WATCH IT! ALL SIDES!" Kurta called out to the others, but they were already in the thick of it.

He whirled around and saw The Pole blazing away with his Ithaca, dropping ranks of sluggos that charged in, drooling and delusional. Mooney was doing the same with his M4, emptying a clip right into the advancing horde.

But where was the kid? The kid?

Kurta raised his Ithaca and dropped a woman whose face was palpitating like the stinger of a wasp. He erased her throat and her head nearly fell off as she tumbled over. There was the kid. He'd become separated, off to the left, near the entrance to PacSun. But he was showing real control, real courage. Firing a three-round burst, pivoting, firing again, repeating the process. Not panicking at all.

Four of them charged Kurta and he went into action.

He fired the riot gun again and again, getting splashed with sluggo gore as skulls flew apart and chests imploded. A slug inched up his leg and he flicked it away, smashing it to slime and gristle under his boot.

"Hit it!" The Pole said as he tossed an incendiary grenade. A half-dozen advancing slugheads were consumed in a cloud of burning white phosphorus.

More poured in and it was pretty much every man for himself.

Kurta ran out of shot and clubbed two sluggos aside as a third took hold of him. He pulled his Colt Python .357 and shot the one in the kneecap and cored the other in the face.

But there were more, always more.

Flames were everywhere, smoke rising in a blinding haze. It was like trying to fight in a fogbank. The others were vague shadows and Kurta was afraid to fire and hit one of them.

A trio of slugheads came out of the smog, two men and one woman, living, pocked zombies nursing huge slug-sacks at their bellies. He didn't bother going for their heads, he clipped all three right in their slugs.

Screaming, disoriented, they contorted and smashed into one another, blood gushing from their bellies as they tried with manically scrambling fingers to repair their destroyed riders.

They were the ideal hosts—they didn't care about themselves, only their parasites.

All around Kurta there was gunfire and shouting, frantic voices calling over the headset, but he couldn't tell from which direction they were coming. It was all surreal, nightmarish, absolute pandemonium.

A woman leaped out at him.

She was naked, tumescent, her skin purple-black. As one hand covered her rider, the other went for Kurta's face. He jammed the .357 in the direction of her foaming mouth and pulled the trigger. At such close range, her face literally split in half, blood and tissue exploding and spraying in every which direction. For one split second after he fired, he saw the bloody skull beneath her skin grinning at him and then she went down at his feet.

There was nothing left to do.

He ran.

22

West looked for Kurta as he slapped another magazine into his M4, firing immediately into the face of a sluggo that was missing much of the top of its head. As he did so, four others came vaulting out at him and one of the exterminators must have been near because he heard the sound of an Ithaca firing and two of the sluggos seemed to explode with putrescence right in front of him. They literally came apart, splashing him with meat, juice, and a greasy tangle of intestines.

A slughead kid grabbed his arm and darted in like a shark, biting down. He felt the pain, but there was no way her teeth could pierce the Tyvek material. He punched her in the head three times before she fell away. She looked up at him with glimmering eyes, lips pulled back from gnashing teeth and he kicked her in the face.

He called out over the headset for the others and voices called back, but where the hell were they?

"Gamestop!" he heard Kurta calling. *"Gamestop!"*

West knew where that was. It was back behind him, towards Kohl's, sandwiched between California Nails and T-Mobile. He knocked two slughead kids aside and started running, or attempting to in his biosuit.

"Hurry!" he heard Kurta say.

"Coming, chief! I'm on my way—"

Something slammed into him, knocking him into the doorway of Sephora. A big sluggo stood there. Naked and well-muscled, he was covered in glistening gore. He clutched his slug tightly, lovingly. It seemed to be breathing, swelling with a sound of stretched, wet rubber, then deflating.

He reached down and West drilled him with a three-round burst that opened up his chest, blood flying in gouts. He staggered back right into three other approaching slugheads and then a tongue of flame shot out of the haze and the lot of them went up like Guy Fawkes dummies. Covered in burning liquid, their eyeballs burst from their sockets. He could hear the hissing of their blood boiling in their veins.

Whoever it was—Mooney or The Pole—was gone.

West got to his feet, stumbling forward through clouds of smoke, fires guttering around him. Behind him, there was an explosion and slugheads were screaming.

Before him, he saw a wall of sluggos advancing. He turned and darted into the doorway of Claire's, leaping behind a rack of necklaces and pendants. The sluggos moved past the doorway without stopping.

West let out a sigh.

Then several more showed.

Gunfire rang out. He heard people calling. Sluggos shrieking. The Pole shouting obscenities.

He rose up, firing at the approaching slugheads, stumbling out into the mall to fire again. He saw ghostly shapes moving in the smoke. And then...then something happened. There was a flash of light, a rumble of thunder, and he was thrown through the doorway of Sephora as a shock wave slammed into him.

23

Mooney didn't know where the hell anyone was.

The smoke was getting so thick that he couldn't see more than ten feet in any direction. He had his M4 in one hand and the gun assembly of the flamethrower in the other. His headset picked up only static. He was in a bad way and he knew it. He heard sporadic gunfire, voices shouting, and the ever-present insane cries of the sluggos.

His Acrylite bubble *really* was cracked, unlike Spengler's. He had been grabbed by a big slughead and smashed repeatedly into the brick façade outside Forever 21 and with such force that his bubble developed a hairline crack. He wasted the sluggo after he'd been dropped, but the crack wasn't going to go away. There must have been a weakness in the material.

Which means you need to get the hell out of here, he told himself. *Don't worry about the others. Get to the APC and get there now.*

The crack was slight, he knew, but it was most definitely there because now he could smell not only the smoke but the sickening stench of rot, human filth, and, of course, the burning sluggos. The smell of scorched flesh and burnt hair was most pervasive.

He began his march back to Kohl's, burning anything that got in his path. By the time he sighted the store in the building haze, the flamethrower tanks were nearly empty. He saw the fountain and what floated in it.

Jesus, the stink!

He used his last shot of fuel when an emaciated woman came storming out of Yankee Candle, her slug-sack looking as if it must have weighed more than she did. There was green foam bubbling from her mouth. She actually attempted speech in a gurgling, perfectly horrible voice, and by then, Mooney had hosed her down. Like a blazing human candle, she charged him with an amazing velocity, trailing smoke and globs of sputtering fat. She missed him completely, crashing into the wall where she broke apart into burning fragments.

From the flaming ruin of her torso, he saw a shape try to rise up before collapsing back into the sizzling conflagration.

A creeper! I was that close to seeing a creeper birth itself—

Then something hit him and he was tossed sideways, losing his M4 in the process. He tripped and went down.

He clambered to his feet and there was an immense monstrosity standing right in front of him—a woman, or something that had once been a woman. Her gray hide was loose, slopping, and fungal, her face peeling from the skull beneath in a bulging purple-blue mass. A shock of yellow hair sprouted from the top of her skull. She had one filmy yellow eye, the other a scarified pocket of pus.

Mooney went for his sidearm, and she smashed him in the helmet with a huge hand like a bunched catcher's mitt. He went down to his knees and she took hold of him, grabbing him by the tanks of his flamethrower and actually throwing him four or five feet. He smashed into the side of the fountain, face bubble first, the crack widening.

Shit!

She grabbed him by the tanks again and he moved fast, unbuckling the harness. She threw the tanks aside. He came up and fired twice with his Colt 9mm. Whether he hit her or not, he couldn't say. She smashed him in the bubble with her fist. As he was driven down, she hit him three more times, her fist splashing the glass with oozing pink-yellow drainage, some of which trickled inside his helmet, filling it with a putrefying stink.

He got to his feet, squeezed off a shot that went right through her shoulder, then she was on him again, mouth opening and closing, gouts of yellow foam flying from her lips as she screeched at him.

She hit him with her bulk and he was knocked back, falling into the stagnant water of the fountain. He landed atop one of the bloated corpses and it exploded on contact, white mushy flesh spraying in every which direction. He sank right into its putrescence. Somewhere during the process, the Colt was knocked from his hand.

He fought free, splashing and kicking, only to see the mammoth female sluggo towering over him, then he was knocked into the water again. Huge, meaty hands gripped him by the throat and forced him underwater. He fought against them, but they were incredibly strong. The flesh of the arms sloughed off in sheets as he clawed at them with his gloved hands. What was beneath felt porous and pulpy.

Mooney thrashed, screaming out as he rolled in the water with the other corpses. The helmet lights showed him the bobbing, bird-picked faces of the fungous corpses in the water with him.

The hotsuit itself was waterproof, as was the helmet...but now it had been breached by the crack in the face bubble. Water found it—foul, slimy water, a bacterial soup enriched by the drainage of the corpses—and began to trickle in. He could feel it against his face, feel it gathering under his chin.

The woman held him under and would not let go.

It didn't matter how much he fought and clawed and kicked. She bore down on him with her full weight and there was just no way to throw her.

Within seconds, the helmet was beginning to fill.

He was going to drown in it!

No, no, no! Not like this! Not goddamn well like this!

The knife! He fumbled awkwardly underwater for the knife, finally locating it and getting it into his hand. He brought it up, stabbing it into the distended woman. He could feel her jerk with each plunge, but her grip did not weaken. With a final surge of strength, he stabbed up higher, sinking it into her throat. He cut and jabbed and sawed. Her head slumped to one shoulder, that yellow-filmed eye rolling in its socket like a juicy larva in an egg sac.

Her mouth opened, foam gurgling free along with blood and nameless dribbling fluids. She pulled him up, his helmet breaking the water, squeezing his throat tightly...then her body contorted with agonal convulsions and vomit spouted from her mouth in a hot spray. She fell forward on top of him, her spongy face splattered over the face bubble.

Then they sank together.

Mooney fought with everything he had, but his suit was waterlogged, his helmet filling, and her massive dead weight smothered him. Crying out, he managed to lift them both out of the water for two or three seconds. As he did so, he gripped her hair with one gloved fist and it came free in a bunch, her skull rupturing open and releasing a flood of brain flukes that poured over his face bubble.

Screaming, he sank again, the woman's bulk pinning him. The helmet was working its way loose. He felt water flood over his throat and down his chest. But the worst thing, the very worst thing, was that the contaminated water was swimming with flukes—dozens and dozens of them. They were about the size of pollywogs, maybe two inches long, greenish-brown and undulant. They slithered over the face bubble.

Then one squeezed through.

Mooney felt it squirm over his chin. It was seeking the hot warmth of his mouth. As it tried to slide between his lips, he bit it in half, spitting out the fragments. The taste was disgusting. Like biting into raw liver. Its narcotic secretions made his tongue numb, his lips feel like rubber. It was like being shot up with Novocain.

Others were in the helmet then.

As his head thrashed from side to side, he felt one of them wriggle up his left nostril, cold and gelatinous. Another crawled into his ear. A third suctioned itself to his right eye.

But as bad as that was, what was worse was that the woman's slug was free and it was inching its way up his suit. It would find where the helmet was loose and creep in, fastening itself to him.

Mooney screamed, but it did him no good.

In his last moments before he became a drug-addicted zombie, he began to giggle as the flukes took control of his mind and the slug slid into his biosuit.

24

"Kid? Kid? Can you hear me? Are you there?"

Oh, Kurta didn't like this at all. His balls were doing the slow crawl and goosebumps were going right up his spine. As he waited there in the gloomy confines of Gamestop, surrounded by the detritus of a dead society, he wondered why he kept fighting to stay alive. Was it that important? The human race was on the way out and everyone knew it; they were just afraid to face the reality of it. He felt like one of the dinosaurs in *Jurassic Park* or its many sequels *ad nauseum*: he was a creature in a world that no longer had a place for him. He was a relic, a living fossil.

So throw aside your weapons and walk out there, he told himself. But that wasn't feasible because he would be slugified, doomed to be less than he was even now—a draft horse, a beast of burden, a fucking pleasure vehicle to be driven by a slug. There was always the .357. Insert barrel into mouth and call it a day.

So why don't you? You're miserable like everyone else. So do it.

But he didn't.

And why was that? Because of West, because of the kid, because West looked up to him? Because West would find his body and see that he had taken the coward's way out and lose respect for him?

Sure, all of the above. And, worse, the kid will become cynical and angry and pessimistic. There's something good in him, and I can't bear the idea that I might taint it. That he might become like me.

Kurta was getting nothing on the headset now save an occasional inaudible crackling. Could have been one of his boys or it could have been an exterminator from one of the other teams.

The only thing to do, he figured, was to make one more sweep. If he found the kid or the others, he'd get them out of there. Otherwise, he'd make for the APC, radio the major and let him make the call.

Reasonable. Logical.

He loaded the .357 and the Ithaca 37 pump. He'd need all the firepower he could muster. He might just have to blast his way out like some fool in an old horseshit and gunpowder opera.

Wait.

A slughead stumbled by. He—or she, because it was hard to tell—was blackened from napalm, trailing smoke, charred bits dropping off as they went, almost casually, on their way.

So stoned on slug juice they can't even feel the pain.

That made him think about not only his addiction (beaten down, but still dangerous) but the many addictions of the masses. Booze. Drugs. Sex. Always looking for the high that would make you feel better and take away the pain. Good God, the slugs with their vast array of pharmaceuticals were a natural. If there was a niche, nature filled it.

Steeling himself, Kurta stepped out into the mall.

It was showdown time.

25

In Lane Bryant—a place he had never heard of before his current predicament—The Pole could hear the sluggos picking their way towards him through the merchandise that was scattered in every direction. They were like berserk Black Friday shoppers, knocking over displays and tipping over racks, shoving and snarling at each other in their search of that one item they just had to have.

And he was pretty sure what (and *who*) that was.

The store was shadowy, lit only by the flickering fires of the mall itself. The smoky haze in the air was getting thicker, the temperature rising. Inside his biosuit, The Pole was sweating. His back was wet, his flesh greasy against the Tyvek material. He waited there, behind the counter, hoping the slugheads wouldn't find him.

He was pretty sure the others were dead.

His only care right then was to evade the hordes long enough so he could slip out and reach the APC. It was the only thing that kept him going.

Now and again, he heard gunfire from upstairs. That meant someone was still alive up there, still making contact. That boosted his confidence. The idea of being the last one in the mall with possibly hundreds of sluggos…oh Christ, that was just too much.

They were getting closer.

He could hear them grunting and growling, making positively repulsive breathing noises that made it sound as if their throats were full of wet leaves.

The Pole didn't know how much was left in the tanks of his flamethrower, but it couldn't have been much the way he'd been splashing around the fire. He figured there was enough for one last spray. When the slugheads got close, he was going to barbecue their asses all at the same time.

Come on then, you fucks, he thought at them. *If you want it that bad, come and get it.*

He hated the idea of wasting juice cooking them, but he knew they weren't going to give him much of a choice. They were real pricks that way—once they got on the trail of something tasty, nothing but death could stop them.

They were about fifteen feet away now, snarling at one another, gnashing their teeth, and making the most dreadful slobbering sounds.

Enough.

He couldn't take it anymore.

He stood up from behind the counter and the slugheads saw him right away.

"COME AND GET IT!" he taunted them.

Baring their teeth, they knocked racks of clothing asunder and stormed in.

The Pole pressed the trigger on the flamethrower gun and a spout of brilliant yellow-white fire shot out and engulfed them. He hosed them down and they danced about, screeching and melting inside their own skins. The flames blazed bright, cremating them down to crumbling scarecrows. They fell into a central heap, twitching and breaking apart, the last of the moisture in them hissing out as steam. To all sides, merchandise was licked with fire, the front of the store building into a great bonfire.

Better get out while you can.

And then, behind him, he heard commotion.

He turned and saw a man stumbling drunkenly in his direction. Another goddamn sluggo bearing down on him…except he wasn't.

In fact, The Pole wasn't sure what the hell he was doing.

He was a tall dude, naked and unpleasant to look upon, his body a map of purple-black contusions, pustulating red sores, and a weird yellowish vein networking that branched like lightning. His slug-sack was blown up like the belly of a woman in her 9th month.

Mr. Sluggo was in a bad way.

His eyes were like balls of oozing black taffy, green foam bubbling from his mouth and nostrils in great, gummy curds. He clawed out frantically in all directions, groaning and gurgling.

The Pole made to toast him…then hesitated.

What the hell was going on?

He'd never seen anything like this before.

What the fuck?

The guy had no hair, his face split open with jagged cracks. His tongue lolled from his lips like a black, oily flap. He opened his mouth and screamed with a high shrieking sound like a screech owl at midnight. He shook. He jerked. His body whipsawed with rapid convulsions. His slug-sack pulsed faster and faster like a madly beating heart. There was a yolky, wet sound and his eyes blew from their sockets in snotty masses of optic jelly. Blood streamed from both nostrils, inky fluid splashing from his mouth.

And then—he cracked open like an egg, everything inside him pushing out in a sluicing expulsion of tissue, organ, entrails, and steaming blood. He hit the floor, breaking apart into an oozing, jellied putrescence.

As he did so, his slug-sack made a crackling sound, bursting like a placenta in a loathsome outpouring of slime and mucid rot.

And then…then The Pole saw it.

The one thing he figured no one else had ever seen.

The birth of a creeper.

It pushed out with a shearing, snapping sort of noise as it molted free of its birth case. He saw it emerge…a creeping pestilence that nearly destroyed his mind. It was probably two feet in length, segmented like a millipede, a brilliant, glistening scarlet. It was broad and fleshy in the front, big around as a man's forearm, tapering to a wiggling vermiform shape at its posterior. It crawled free on legs that were not legs at all but slender tentacles, smooth and suckerless and coiling.

It moved forward, then paused, watching him with black beady eyes—six of them. There were four tentacle-like feelers reaching from its head, but these were segmented. And it had a mouth, an oval puckering hole that expanded as wide as a coffee can with each breath it took, like a catfish gasping for air, its entire body inflating likewise.

Each time it did, The Pole could see right down its throat into its gut. It had no teeth, only a tongue-like appendage that was hollow as a tube.

This was it.

This was fucking it.

This is what the larval slugs became—worming, insect-like creatures with tentacle legs, *creepers*. Each was full of eggs, reproducing (Dr. Dewarvis said) by a form of parthenogenesis, literally born pregnant. It would lay eggs, possibly hundreds of them, and from each would be born a wiggler with an attendant brood of endoparasitic flukes (neither of which could survive without the other, forming a sort of mutualism). The wiggler would attach itself to a host, releasing immature flukes into the host's body that would migrate to the brain and hijack its nervous system with a devastating chemical dependency. As the host gorged itself on any meat available, building up protein reserves, the slug would drain nutrients and the flukes would thrive in the human brain. The slug needed the flukes to subjugate the host. The flukes required the slug to find a host. Ectoparasite and endoparasite in symbiotic union. Once the host was reduced to a mindless servitor, the slug would mature and birth itself, molting to a creeper—by then the host was little more than walking carrion—and the entire ugly life cycle would begin again.

The creeper studied The Pole.

It recognized an enemy that would have to be vanquished. He could feel its black, penetrating eyes boring into him, not necessarily intelligent but certainly not stupid either. *Cruel,* The Pole decided. *Arrogant.* All warm-blooded life forms existed to be subjugated and exploited by it.

It really was a fascinating, unique creature just as Doc Dewarvis had said.

So, The Pole did what came natural to him: he burned it.

It writhed and flopped in the consuming envelope of napalm. When it finally died, it went black as cinders. Liquid sizzled out of it, then it cracked open like a hot chestnut.

"Goddamn," The Pole said to himself. "Ain't that just something?"

26

"KID! HEY, KID! HEY, FUCKING WEST, WHERE THE HELL ARE YOU?"

Kurta's voice echoed through the mall corridor. He got no response over the headset and picked up absolutely nothing on his external mic, save the shrill cries of the sluggos. The smoke was so thick now it was like fog. It hid him from the sluggos, but it also hid them from him.

He ducked behind a dead potted tree as two dark and menacing forms swept past him.

That's it. Go on your merry way, assholes.

He had left Gamestop and was making a final run through Ex-3's sector of the mall. If he found anyone alive or injured, he'd drag them out with him. If they were dead, he'd log it.

But not West.

Jesus Christ, not the kid.

Kurta had no idea what was going on, but he was getting attached to him. It was strange. He didn't know if it was a fatherly thing or a brotherly thing, but he was feeling very protective of him.

Like Stiv.

Sure, he'd loved that sonofabitch down deep, too. But that had been different. He admired Stiv with his fuck-you attitude and his complete contempt for authority. His personal philosophy was even more cynical than Kurta's. Stiv believed that human beings were basically greedy, self-indulgent pigs. Things like loyalty and honor were a pipe dream…oh, people could be both loyal *and* honorable when it served their ends, but not unless it did. People hated him at the bunker for his beliefs and how he'd laugh uncontrollably when they spoke of faith or a higher power.

But for all that, for all his recklessness and pessimism, he had balls like Kurta had never seen before. He feared nothing and no one. Everything had been black-and-white for Stiv.

But what about West?

Kurta wondered if he'd been hurting over Stiv for so long that he'd just grabbed the next young guy who came along and made him a proxy.

Maybe.

Maybe not.

West had potential. He was basically good, dependable, and trustworthy. And naïve. Christ, was he was naïve. But you had to like him and something about him made you want to do right by him. Maybe it was more than that. Maybe it was that he reminded Kurta of himself before he totally fucked his life up with drugs and bad choices.

Regardless, he wasn't leaving West behind.

He either brought the kid out alive and breathing or he confirmed his death. That was a given.

I'll find you, kid. See if I don't.

27

Mooney came out of dormancy like a switch being thrown. Like a 100-kilowatt generator being cold-cranked to life. Light—a dirty, dingy, awful sort of light—flooded his chemically dependent brain and it only served to illuminate the skulking, grinning things hiding in the corners. He screamed in his head and the things came for him, slithering forward and sinking their red-stained teeth into the shivering meat of his mind.

GET OUT! GET OUT! he cried. *GET OUT OF ME! GET OUT OF MY HEAD!*

But they weren't leaving; he had friends for life.

Part of him sank into the narcotic bliss of nonentity, nonexistence, and nothingness brought about by the flukes setting up house in his brain. Another part, struggling, winking out like a distant star, realized that it had not only lost the battle but lost the war. It rose up fierce and defiant one last time, then—

Then it was gone.

Crushed like an insect.

Something took its place. He was rebooted. New software wrote over the old Mooney, depositing all that he had been directly into the trash bin.

He suddenly felt at peace in a way he had never known before. He felt calm. He had a sense of purpose and a sense of belonging that was alien but wonderful. There were no more battles being fought inside him, no conflicting emotions, no unanswered questions, no moral and ethical ambiguity. Everything was beautifully black-and-white. He was what he was in a way that was meant to be.

The waters were no longer muddied; they were clear.

There was instinct.

There was need.

But there was very little else.

Save the consuming desire to protect the thing that had spun a cocoon at his belly with his own flesh and fat. It was his center, his all, his reason for being. If was a gift that he must mother, feed, and protect.

And it was hungry.

And because it was hungry, *he* was hungry.

As long as he kept it safe, warm, and fed, it would reward him with the ambrosia of dopamine spikes via the flukes. If he failed in his duty, the slug would cut him off and the deprivation would not only fill his guts with hot knife blades, it would turn his brain to sludge from the accumulated toxins and waste materials of the flukes who would run rampant and unchecked through his gray matter.

These were things Mooney knew without consciously knowing them. They were now part of his natural rhythms.

But for now…

FOOD! He wanted FOOD! He craved FOOD! He had to find it, secure it, fill himself with it. It was the only thing that mattered.

Even now his slug, which was small and pulsing in its womb beneath his ever-present hand, was directly uplinked with the flukes. Together, they had hijacked not only his biochemistry but his nervous system which they used to communicate in their own fashion.

And what they wanted, *he* wanted.

Mooney moved through the mall, his heightened animal instinct guiding him to FOOD. He was now in the sector that

Ex-2 had fought for before being overwhelmed. Casting his helmet aside, he discovered two of his brother slugheads feeding on a dead exterminator. He joined them, shoving sweet globs of belly fat into his mouth and chewing them with carnal satisfaction. As the food reached his stomach, its nutrients were siphoned off by his slug which, even then, was growing at an alarming rate.

As he filled himself, he was rewarded, feeling better with each swallow.

Then the flukes cut him off and he began to crash.

He needed more.

He had to have more.

And in the shadowy runs of his brain, he knew a way to achieve this.

The hot suit of the exterminator lying at his feet, that which wasn't spattered red, reminded him that there were others. His instinctively hated them. But at the same time, he knew they were FOOD. He would find them and feed on them.

But they were dangerous.

He would have to be cunning.

He started the long walk back to the other end of the mall. Along the way, he saw his helmet and put it on.

Now they would accept him.

His stomach growled.

His slug purred happily at his belly.

The flukes gorged themselves on his brain tissue.

And he was content…but hungry.

28

Janis D was the only survivor of Ex-5. All the others were slugified or dead. She had crawled into Tony Roma's on the second level, leaving a blood trail behind her that looked—*ha, ha, ha!*—like the smeared slime trail of a slug.

Now ain't that something? she thought. *Ain't that just something?*

Things had gotten hot and heavy.

Real hot and heavy.

The sluggos were everywhere on level two. Within ten minutes of staging, Five made contact. They gunned down a dozen slugheads and torched twenty more. Then the sluggos came from everywhere—Red Lobster and Romano's Macaroni Grill, the Longhorn Steak House and Ruby Tuesday's. They were everywhere and in unbelievable numbers. Five emptied magazine after magazine, spent round after round after round. They emptied both flamethrowers, but it still wasn't enough.

Janis D called Ex-2 for backup.

Two charged up the dead escalator and ran into a wall of sluggos coming down to greet them.

Rounds flew.

Grenades were thrown.

The floors were greasy with blood and viscera. As the last few valiant exterminators in full retreat fought a losing rear-guard action, the sluggos (driven to maniacal levels) dove off the railings on top of them.

The survivors of Two were buried alive and torn literally to pieces.

With all that lead flying, somebody was bound to get drilled by friendly fire. Janis D just didn't think it was going to be her. Not until some scattershot took out her left kneecap.

Now they were coming for her.

She had made it into Tony Roma's—damn, for a minute there she thought she could still smell the ribs but it was only the roasted smell of burning bodies—and managed to get a pressure bandage on her knee, shooting herself up with antibiotics and morphine. Between the latter and the trauma, she was going in and out of consciousness.

As she peered around the corner out into the mall, she saw a good thirty or forty slugheads crawling in her direction. They were following her blood trail, sniffing it like dogs. Backlit by the raging fires behind them, clouds of black smoke churning in the air, body parts cast about, it looked like a medieval vision of Hell out there.

They would have her.

Or would they?

As the first ones came through the door of Tony Roma's, as voracious as any customers that had ever come for the baby back ribs, Janis D knew there was no surviving this.

They would gut her.

They would skin her and feast on her organs, suck up her salty blood and snap her bones for the creamy marrow within.

She studied the ruined faces and slavering mouths of the pack, bare feet from her now.

As they made to take hold of her, she played a little trick on them. Something she had seen in an old WWII movie with Mickey Rooney. When he was surrounded by the enemy, wounded and unable to move, old hard-bitten Marine Mickey had played a joke.

So she followed suit.

When they grabbed her, she pulled the pins on her last two grenades.

And closed her eyes.

Right before they went off and took seven or eight sluggos with them to the promised land, she thought about Kurta. He'd always been the best, exterminating more slugheads than anyone else.

Oh yeah, Kurt? Beat this!

Then the grenades exploded.

29

West came awake to a sensation of being petted like a dog. Of a hand stroking him gently, running up and down his chest with a slow, gentle motion that made him want to sink back down into dreamless sleep. There was a vague memory in his mind of his mother doing the same thing to him when he'd had a bad dream.

Except that his mom had died when he was fourteen.

And he was not home, not in his bed. In fact, he was—

Where?

He couldn't be sure. But as his mind gradually climbed the steep hill to full consciousness, a sense of panic woke inside him as did physical pain. An awful throbbing in his legs and belly.

What? What? *What?*

Slowly, infinitely slowly, a sense of where he was and where he was not came back to him. He blinked. His eyes focused. He licked his dry lips. He tried to move, but the pain in his guts and legs kept him still.

As terror surged hot in his belly, he realized he was being held…and worse, *what* held him.

He heard a gurgling noise.

Fine droplets of something dark and muddy dripped onto his face bubble.

There had been an explosion. He knew that much. It had blown him into the store, into Sephora…and this thing had found him.

Through his bubble, he saw a scaly, mottled hand. Its ring finger was missing which made it look like the yellow claw of a bird. It brushed against the Acrylite of the bubble, then it resumed stroking his chest.

He wanted to scream.

But he didn't dare.

The slughead that held him was making no threatening moves. He was like some big, much-loved doll to it. And the slughead—a woman, *something* like a woman—was a child mothering over it.

Dear Christ, she was even making cooing sounds.

Cooing sounds that were somehow slurping and liquid.

The store was semi-illuminated by a guttering orange light from the fires. There was also a dull yellow light from his helmet. He hated it, because as he shifted his head slightly, it showed him the woman in detail.

She was a monster.

There was no getting around that. He had seen some perfectly horrible-looking sluggos, but never anything like this. She looked like some quivering fetal rat, embryonic and unformed. Her skin was a sheer yellow membrane, oddly transparent. He could actually see her veins and arteries delivering blood, flexing quilts of muscle, a jutting architecture of bone. There were only a few scraggly, spine-like hairs on her head. The skull was long and narrow, set forward on the neck, the eye sockets huge, the nose pushed in, the jaw pushed out.

He tried not to completely lose it.

He was shaking inside his hot suit, damp with chill and sweat.

She brought her revolting face in closer, appraising him with glassy, immense eyes that were unblinking and fishlike. Something squeezed its way out of her nose and dropped to the helmet bubble: a squirming fluke. She plucked it up quickly, sucking it between her lips. The sound of her chewing it brought his stomach into his throat.

Not now, not now, a voice in his head warned him. *Don't you dare throw up now.*

He was hurt bad. He knew that. It must have been a grenade that got him. If that was the case, then his legs and maybe even his belly had shrapnel in it. But that still didn't explain why this fucking sluggo was…well, *nursing* him, for lack of a better word. She should have been trying to tear him apart, to feed on him.

Yet, as hideous as she was, she was being almost loving to him.

He tried to regulate his breathing. His legs, particularly the right one, were really starting to hurt. They felt wet which meant he must have been bleeding pretty bad. If he laid here too long, he might bleed right out. But his rifle was gone. There was still the knife at his left hip and the .9mm at his right…at least, he hoped so. The gun was the thing. But he had to get it out without startling his keeper. If she felt threatened, she'd probably rip him apart.

She was still cooing.

He inched his hand towards the holster. The gun was still there. He waited, then popped the catch. She made a low snarling sound in her throat. She'd heard it all right. She brought her yellow, sunken face closer to the bubble. Through her membranous flesh, he could see her abnormal skull grinning at him.

Jesus, this was going to be touchy.

She stroked him, cooing and gurgling, watching the entrance of Sephora for activity. Now and again, she would cock her head as if she had heard something, her body tensing…then she'd relax.

West slid the .9mm out with infinite slowness, not more than an inch at a time. When he finally had it almost free, he heard approaching footsteps. The slughead went stiff and trembling like a cat that has sighted a bird. She growled low in her throat like a watchdog. She looked at him and then at the figure approaching the entrance. She began making hissing sounds. She pulled herself up in a crouch and West slid off her lap with a jolt of agony in his legs.

He grimaced, trying not to cry out, but a groan escaped his lips. He saw the huge fleshy sack at her belly visibly palpitate.

The sluggo, as if finally realizing he was a living thing and *food,* screeched and tore at him.

West screamed.

He tried to get the gun out and dropped it—

30

"Kid," Kurta cried out when he saw West, putting the tactical light of his Ithaca on him *and* the mutant horror that was attacking him.

The sluggo screeched.

Kurta didn't hesitate. He fired, racked the pump, and fired again. The slughead seemed to explode, gore splattering against a still-standing rack of bath soaps. Blood and meat rained down on West, who was crying out in disgust or pain or maybe both.

Kurta charged in there.

He saw the woman's slug burst free from its sheath and crawl up West's leg. He set his riot gun aside, and snatched the slug in his hands. It writhed like a snake, twisting and turning, putting out slippery jelly. He nearly dropped it. As he made to give it a toss, it wrapped around his left fist and spat gobs of goo onto his face bubble that splatted like soft hailstones. They tried to root themselves to the glass and he brushed them away, leaving a smear.

The slug would not let go so he gripped it in both fists and squeezed it with everything he had, clenching his teeth and bearing down. It made an awful whirring sound as it bulged to the bursting point…then it exploded in his hands, erupting with slime and meaty tissue. He tossed its flaccid, dead remains aside. It looked like a rubbery, burst balloon.

Kurta's face bubble was thick with gore.

He fumbled around, finding a drapery and wiping the slimy remains free.

"You okay?" he asked West.

"Not great," West admitted, outlining everything that had happened.

"Probably The Pole. Had to be The Pole."

"Mooney?"

Kurta shook his head. "No, kid. He's dead. I found him floating in the fountain with a dead sluggo."

"Dammit. I liked him."

"Yeah, so did I."

Kurta still had his medical bag. He applied clotting agent to West's legs—the right one was the worst of the two—and bandaged them up, gave him a shot of antibiotics. But no painkiller.

"Sorry, kid, but I can't have you nodding off on me. I need your eyes." He packed his medical bag back up. Like his guns, it was the one thing he dared never leave behind. "You got shrapnel in there, man. Nothing in your belly, though. Skin's not even broken. You must have been punched by some flying debris."

"I'm not gonna lose a leg, am I?"

"No, I don't think so. We get back to the bunker, they'll put you out, clean the metal out of you."

West relaxed a bit. "How are we gonna get out of here?"

"We're going to walk. At least," Kurta said, "I am. You're going piggyback."

Inside his helmet, West shook his head. "I can't let you do that. It'll put you at risk."

"You don't have a choice."

"But—"

"Just leave it to me, kid."

31

West had an idea.

Since Kurta insisted on being used as a sedan chair, he wanted to make it easier on both of them. He'd worked at a big mall in Pittsburgh. Functionally, they were all pretty much the same, he explained to Kurta. The electrical, plumbing, telecom lines etc. were run in mechanical shafts beneath the floor.

"If we can find one of the maintenance sites, there should be access to the shafts."

"Then what?"

"Then we follow them under the mall. They'll lead to access hatches set in the sidewalks outside for utility workers," West said. "You've probably seen them a hundred times at malls. You've probably walked over them."

Kurta liked it.

It would be a good way out. The chances of running into slugheads down there would be minimal. Once they were outside, it would be easy to get to one of the APCs.

"Okay," he said. "What's the best place to look?"

West told him that a mall the size of Southgate should have several maintenance sites. The best place to look would be in one of the corridors that led away from the stores, the ones where the restrooms were located. That's where the maintenance sites would be along with storerooms, janitorial closets etc.

Kurta nodded. "All right. I'll be back soon as I can. Keep out of sight."

"You can count on it."

32

The Pole was filled with self-congratulations because he was such a wily, sneaky cuss.

As far as he knew, he was the last living member of Ex-3. Five and Two were fucking worm food by then.

There was only him; no one else.

Instead of dying below like the others, he decided to reach the outside from *above.* He'd found a maintenance crawlway with a ladder. He assumed it would reach right to the roof. Instead, interestingly enough, it terminated above Red Lobster. It was a service shaft leading up to the catwalks and rafters.

At first, he'd thought: *Ahh, oh shit. This is no good.*

Then a little light went on inside his brain—*well, why not? Crawl along the rafters, keep going until you reach the catwalk just beneath the skylights. Open one of them and crawl out onto the roof. That's a start. A real good start. And you avoid the hordes below.*

He was proud of himself.

Maybe that goddamn Kurta had been a good leader and a real ass-kicker. Maybe Mooney had been smart and knew everything about anything. And maybe Spengler had just been born lucky.

Sure, and maybe The Pole didn't have any of those things in great supply, but what he *did* have was common sense and good instincts.

He was way up there now, but it was no biggie. Heights had never bothered him. Slinking his way along the rafters, knocking a few stray birds' nests aside, he had a pretty good view of not just the ground floor but the second floor.

And, Jesus, they were lousy with slugheads.

Hundreds? Sure, he didn't think that was too much of an exaggeration. It would have taken some real balls, some real luck, and some real planning to get through that gauntlet.

No wonder the others were dead.

It's the best thing you could have hoped for, Kurta. The very best thing. Because sooner or later, it was gonna be war between us and you knew it like I knew it.

There was no doubt of that in The Pole's mind. And when war came, he could be a real crafty SOB. It wouldn't have been a face-to-face battle. No sir, Kurta was too mean for that honorable hero shit. He wasn't a guy you wanted to take on like that. No, The Pole had it all worked out—he would have stabbed that high and mighty prick right in the back.

Not that it mattered now.

God, the smoke was thick up here and the heat was fucking unbearable. The filter on his mask was keeping most of it out, but it couldn't do squat for the heat. In his biosuit, he felt like a wiener in a bun being slow-roasted.

But not far, not far now. Catwalk is only thirty feet away. You can make it. Keep your eye on the prize.

Now and again, the smoke cleared and he could see the sluggos below. Some of them were on fire. Others were stumbling about like they were almost dead. Still others, on the upper level, were picking at the bones of Five.

He began to crawl faster before he was overwhelmed by the heat or lost his nerve because of what he was seeing below. It all reminded him a little too much of his days in Catholic school. When Father Petakis had described the torments of Hell to them in fourth grade, this is almost exactly the sort of thing that The Pole had pictured in his impressionable mind.

Just get to that catwalk or you're going to die up here. The birds'll pick you down to the bones.

And it was this image more than anything that really got him moving. For he could see it with a surreal sort of clarity in his mind: the shrunken hotsuit tangled in the rafters, yellowed bones poking out of it at right angles, the bird's nests built in his ribcage, his skull offering a leering grin behind the face bubble.

Coughing on the bad air in the helmet, he got closer to the catwalk and the freedom it offered.

33

Ducking away from slugheads, the smoke thicker than ever in the mall as the fires blazed out of control, Kurta figured if they didn't get out and get out soon, they never would.

As he worked his way down past Hot Topic, heading for the corridor at the next turn that would take him to the bathrooms and hopefully what he sought, a couple sluggos appeared out of the smoke. He pulled back, ducking into the doorway of Torrid before they saw him.

And it was then that something took hold of him from behind.

Not just took hold of him, but dropped down on him.

Shit!Shit!Shit!Shit!Shit!Shit!

It was on his back, gripping his neck with something that felt like metal tongs through the biosuit. It squeezed and squeezed as other things crawled over his spine like coiling worms.

With a cry, he dropped the Ithaca and went down to his knees. He reached back, hands scrabbling in a frenzy to peel that weight off his back, that undulating mass.

But it clung tenaciously.

Through the gloves, he could not tell what it was but in his rioting imagination, it was every horror spawned in the hellzone of a slug-infested world. He could not seem to get a grip on it nor a proper feel for what it was. It was firm and rippling, a living sheath of muscle.

Then he saw its reflection in the plate glass windows of Torrid.

A creeper.

There was a fucking creeper on his back.

Beyond panic, he jumped to his feet despite the pain at his neck. Without hesitating, he threw himself backwards, crushing the creeper between his suit and the brick façade outside the store. It gave out a piping sort of cry like a tree frog, but did not loosen its hold. He kept bashing it into the wall again and again, using every ounce of strength he had and all of his weight. Finally, on the sixth or seventh try, he heard a sharp sort of snapping sound. The creeper let out a high, trilling cry, its legs bicycling madly against the back of his suit with a very unpleasant slithery sort of sound.

Got you, you prick! I fucking well got you!

The grip at his neck weakened considerably. He reached behind him, grasped the quivering mass and peeled it free, whipping it at the wall with everything he had.

It made another snapping sound as it struck.

It flopped manically on the floor, trilling and squeaking now, one of its segments clearly damaged, cracked open like a peanut shell, a yellow soupy fluid leaking from it. Its tentacle-like legs scrambled for purchase, but it was bent, crooked, and it couldn't seem to propel itself forward or get into a defensive or fighting posture (if it even had such a thing).

Kurta stared down at it with an undeniable sense of triumph.

It kept trying to pull away from him, knowing it was in serious trouble, but the best it could manage was a sideways lurching motion, a trail of that sticky yellow sap left in its wake.

Finally, as if realizing it could not escape its fate, it raised its fore end off the floor, breathing rapidly and almost convulsively. What Kurta was seeing was pretty much what The Pole had—a shiny, blood-red arthropod, centipede-like, its looping appendages like something from a sea creature; the mouth yawning open with each gulp of air, revealing a ribbed, tunnel-like throat that led to its gut; the slithering mouth tendrils; and the perfectly awful black marbles of its eyes.

It had to die.

It was a living mass of eggs and Kurta knew it.

Just one of these things was enough to infect a city.

Just one. It would lay its eggs somewhere moist and warm, and from each would emerge a larval wiggler that would become a parasitic slug which, in time, would molt into a creeper like this one—capable of laying hundreds of more eggs.

The big problem with these damn things besides the obvious, Kurta could recall Dr. Dewarvis saying, *is that they have no natural enemies. The entire mammal kingdom is their host and their food. How are you supposed to stop something like this if nature won't even lend you a hand?*

How right he was.

These things were infesting the globe, completely unchecked save for the exterminators, and the idea of that, of mankind being brought to its knees and ultimate extinction because of an ugly crawly horror like this was not just repulsive, it was offensive.

Kurta drew his .357 Python and blew the creeper away. It left a splash of yellow snot sprayed over the plate glass of Torrid. Split wide, its head was a macerated ruin. Drainage bubbled free. Its hind section convulsed one last time and released a gummy translucent emulsion filled with hundreds of eggs that looked like frog spawn.

Picking up his Ithaca, Kurta, more than a little weak in the knees, resumed his journey.

34

The skylight panels were hinged, so it was fairly easy for The Pole to boost himself up through one of them and climb out into the fresh air. Then he began snaking his way over the top of the skylights themselves. He was certain they would support his weight, but to be on the safe side, he kept the catwalk beneath him at all times.

Within five minutes, he was free of it and on the actual roof of the Southgate Mall. Good God, it was a rolling landscape of roofs, rising, falling, jutting and convex. There were seagulls up there and crows and ravens. Bird shit everywhere.

And bones.

The bones of animals and humans. The birds must have been carrying things up here to feed upon.

He stripped his helmet off even though it was against the rules to do so in a hot zone.

Fuck it.

The air was fresh, as fresh as air can be with the stink of bird poo, dander, rotting things, and the smell of human remains wafting up from the parking lot. Regardless, after having his head stuck in the helmet for hours and breathing filtered air, it smelled wonderful.

It was cool, fresh and cool.

When he looked behind him, he could see the smoke escaping from the skylight he'd left open.

It was going to be an inferno in there in an hour or so. All that dusty, dry merchandise was going to go up fast. Which was a good reason to find a way off the roof.

He made it to the southern edge, but that was no good. It was a sheer drop of seventy feet to the parking lot.

Now wouldn't that just be ironic if I couldn't get down?

35

"This is it," Kurta said under his breath. "Exactly what I was looking for."

He was in one of the maintenance rooms. It was a pretty big place with a detailed map of the mall on the wall. A few desks covered with dusty papers and dead laptops. There was a storeroom with tools in cribs. Another room with a wall of electronic equipment that he guessed was the mall's broadband hub. The thing that interested him was an elevator cage that apparently led to the mechanical shaft below.

The sight of it made his heart sink.

An elevator was no good without electricity.

Then, relieved, he found a man-sized conduit with a ladder bolted to the wall that led down.

He decided to have a look-see.

If there were slugheads down there, better to face them now than when he was piggybacking West.

It was an easy climb down and he panned about with the tactical light of his riot gun. The passage went on farther than his light could reach. It looked empty. He heard no sounds.

Take a look. A good long look.

So he did. He moved down the passage for about a hundred feet, maybe more, until it branched to the left and right. He went to the right for about another forty feet, then it branched again.

Shit.

It was a maze down there. Maybe back in the day when the lights were still working it might have made some sense, but now it was all pretty spooky. He could just about imagine wandering endlessly down there until he gave up, crawling into a corner to die.

Melodramatics, that's all.

Maybe West would know, maybe he'd be able to make some sense of it. That's when Kurta decided he wasn't using his bean. The passages snaked all over the place beneath the mall because they had to. What he needed to do was to think about where he was in the mall itself and then move in that direction and that should terminate with one of the access hatches West was talking about.

But that wasn't for now.

Now he had to get West down here and that would be a job in of itself.

He cut back down to the ladder, feeling good about the fact that he'd seen no sluggos down there. He moved quickly up the rungs. In his mind, it was all so simple now if only it would work out. If only they could get out of there and to the APC without incident. Up in the maintenance room, he went back to the door, peered around and saw no one in the corridor.

The smoke was thick. He could feel the heat building as he passed the hallways leading to the restrooms.

And that's when he saw a white blur come out of the darkness. It slammed into him. Hard. His knees buckled from the impact and the Ithaca hit the floor, sliding away.

Fuck!

A woman came charging out at him. She was on him before he could clear the .357 from its holster. He saw little of her before she hit him again. She was naked with very large breasts, reddish hair plastered to her face, and mottled gray skin. That was all he saw.

Then she hit him and he saw stars again.

She jumped on him, piggybacking him, legs scissored around his waist, her hands clawing at his throat as if they were trying to dig their way through the Tyvek material. This was even worse than the creeper. She kept saying something in a low, cracked voice and it took him a moment or two to realize it was, *"Piss, piss, piss! Pissy piss piss!"*

It might have been darkly comic if she hadn't been trying her damnedest to get him down where she could kill him.

He whirled around, bucking and jerking, trying to throw her. Every time he tried to get his gun or knife out, she clawed madly at his arm, pinning it and nearly twisting it out of the socket.

She wasn't too heavy—he couldn't imagine that she weighed more than 120 pounds. But in the hotsuit, in the heat and smoke, it was just too damn much. His legs were giving way, the strength running from him.

Making squealing and croaking sounds, she kept batting at his helmet. He slammed her against the wall, but she clung that much tighter. Finally, stumbling about drunkenly, he tripped over a bench and they both went down.

Then she had him.

Effortlessly, it seemed, she pinned him, straddling him, still clawing at his face bubble as if she just couldn't understand the nature of this barrier that separated her nails from his face. Gouts of foam and slime and some sort of yellow ooze like egg yolk hung from her mouth. Her eyes were horribly bloodshot, set in livid purple sockets.

He got the .357 out after a good struggle and nearly got the barrel to her head, but she batted it away. He tried again and she knocked it away just as fast.

He didn't bother with anything fancy then.

He cracked her in the side of the head with the butt. She let out a short little exclamation of surprise and he threw her off. She rolled over and came up, breathing hard. Clots of gore dropped from her nostrils and juiced from her mouth. She was like some heaving bag of carrion. She bared her teeth, cocked her head, squealed out some nonsensical thing, and began to crawl right over to him again.

Her slug-sack was large and stout. It was securely webbed to her belly, sending out dark threads under her skin like rootlets right up into her large, trembling breasts.

As she came on, chattering her teeth and reaching for him, a voice in Kurta's brain said, *you're being attacked by a fucking stripper from Hell.*

He fired twice.

The first round was off and blew a hole through her left shoulder. The second caught her right in the face, the bullet's exit taking out the back of her head. Her brains and blood struck the corridor wall like a handful of greasy, slimy shit, slowing dripping down it in clotted trails.

Kurta got to his feet.

I'm coming, kid, I'm coming.

Hurting, tired, he vanished into the funneling smoke and billowing heat.

36

After forty-five minutes of searching for an egress, The Pole realized that there was no way off the roof. Absolutely no way. The shortest drop was off the arch over the back of the food court where all the little tables were with their rotting canvas umbrellas. And that was still a twenty-foot drop onto the pavement.

In the distance, he could see an APC parked.

It must have belonged to Two.

So close, so close.

At the sight of it, he started shouting at the very top of his lungs: "DIRTY! DIRTY! DIRTY MOTHERFUCKING BULLSHIT! WHY THE FUCK IS ANY OF THIS GODDAMN WELL HAPPENING?" His voice echoed off into the distance, but no one, of course, answered it.

He was alone.

Dreadfully alone.

The sun was beginning to sink into the western sky and it would be dark in a couple of hours and there he waited, most surely screwed, chewed, and barbecued (as they used to say when he was a kid a thousand years before, it seemed).

What now?

What the hell now?

The smell of smoke was strong, even outside. Clouds of it were billowing across the parking lot, being pulled apart by the wind.

Sighing, knowing his rage was just a simple waste of energy, he stepped to the edge of the arch.

No, it was just too far down.

Last thing he needed now was to break a leg or twist an ankle.

It meant he had to go back inside.

Shit!

For a moment, he even thought of leaping fifteen feet through the air to the flagpole and shimmying down it. But he was pretty certain how that would end.

He started back across the mountainous terrain of the roofs. He kept himself oriented as to where the APC was. He had seen several hatches that led back inside the mall. Probably crawlways for the maintenance people to get up top to work on the banks of air conditioners and what not.

He was looking for a hatch as near to the outer wall of the mall as possible.

Ten minutes later, he found one.

It was only about thirty feet from the parking lot and, if luck held, it might have its own doorway leading outside. The hatch was locked from the inside, but he blew it open with his .357. He shined the light down there. Just ladder rungs in the wall leading down to the second floor by the looks of it.

Putting his helmet back on and praying for an act of God, he started down.

37

It took some doing to get West down the ladder into the maze of passages. He was fighting against the pain of shifting his legs, but there was really nothing Kurta could do for him.

"Just hang tight," he told him. "Just hang tight."

Now he had him piggybacked and was moving slowly down the passages. He was just glad West didn't weigh any more than he did. It was tough going at first, but after Kurta's back adjusted to it, it wasn't too bad.

"Next turn," West panted. "I think...I think we should hang left."

Christ, he sounded like shit.

Once they reached the APC and Kurta got him inside, he'd shoot him up with morphine and put him out for the thirty-odd mile drive back to the bunker. It was the best that could be done for him.

Kurta, the Ithaca pump in his hands, led the way forward. With the added bulk of West, he couldn't move too fast. And maybe that was a good thing because they had come too far to fuck this up now.

After ten minutes or so when West had not said anything, Kurta said, "Hey, kid, you still with me?"

"Yeah...yes, sure I am."

Not good. He was getting weak. He needed some real medical care. *C'mon, kid, don't go out on me now.* He had an urge to shift him a little so the pain in his leg would wake him up, but he didn't have the heart to do it.

After panning the left passage with his light, he moved slowly down it. He found a set of bones on the floor dressed in dirty rags. One of them had died down here or maybe it was a human being who'd just offed themselves. The desire to do that was something Kurta understood just fine.

He didn't like to think of how many times he'd contemplated the same.

He paused.

Did I just hear something or is it my own footsteps coming back at me?

Standing there, feeling West's dead weight pressing down on him, feeling very much the rock and the hard place he was trapped between, Kurta heard the sound again.

It was somewhere ahead.

Somewhere the light would not reach.

Question was: did he blunder into it or did he set West down, take care of business, and then come back for him? If he did the former and ran into a real sluggo nest, they were both fucked because there was no way to do any real fighting while he was carrying West. If he did the latter, he left West open to attack.

The sounds ahead were getting louder, echoing down the passages so that he could not truly be sure they *were* ahead of him. Maybe they were behind him or off in one of those side passages.

As the sounds gained volume, Kurta found himself more indecisive than ever before.

He didn't have a choice; he set West down.

He crouched down with him and gently eased him off. He wasn't answering now. He was loose, limp, and sprawling. He slumped over right away, and Kurta had to pull him back up, push him up against the wall in such a way that his own weight would keep him there.

"West?" he said. "West? C'mon, man, answer me."

Nothing.

Shit.

Although they were in a hot zone and the baddies were pushing in, Kurta took off his helmet and then West's. Despite the pressure bandage, there was blood seeping out of the tears in West's suit. Kurta got his bad leg up, brought it across his knees so he could get a look at it, and blood ran out of West's boot.

A lot of blood.

If the pressure bandage couldn't stop the flow, chances were an artery had been nicked and if that was the case, West would never make it back to the bunker. He'd be dead long before they reached it.

"West...West? Can you hear me? Kid...can you hear me?"

West's face in the light was sweat-beaded and pale. It felt hot to the touch. Drool ran out of the corner of his mouth. With his gloves off, Kurta could barely get a pulse. Not only that but his breathing was so shallow it was nonexistent.

He's dying. You know he's dying. He's probably lost too much blood now to stay conscious. He's in shock and death will be next.

What are you going to do about that?

With a sinking feeling of utter despair, Kurta knew there was nothing he could do about it. He wasn't in very good shape himself by that point and the only thing that had kept him going was the idea of getting the kid back to the bunker. That was the light at the end of the tunnel for him.

Now it had been extinguished.

Funny, really, when you thought about it. He'd been strong all day, fighting and killing and barely surviving, and now, when he needed it the most, it just wasn't there. It was gone. Really gone. Giggling, he opened up his suit. He found his cigarettes, lit one, and sat next to West, back up against the wall. They looked like a couple guys kicking back after a long day.

Footsteps were coming.

Kurta still sat there, the Ithaca across his knees. He knew he should get up, but he was just done in, physically and mentally and maybe even spiritually in that his will to fight was gone.

The light reflecting off the opposite wall showed him a shape approaching.

"We're over here," he said.

There was a gurgling noise and a grinding of teeth. A sluggo approached. He supposed it had been a woman once by the breasts, but other than that, it was really hard to tell. She wore her skin like a baggy coat that was splattered with gore and drainage, her eyes glazed white and sightless. She was still deadly even though she couldn't see. By the size of her slug-sack, it was obvious she wasn't long for this world and soon the happy event would be realized: the birth of a creeper.

"Grrrrrghhhhlllllgggg," she muttered, seeming to choke on the greenish foam and pink fluid issuing from her mouth in gobby rivers and dangling ribbons.

"Shit, yes," Kurta said.

Which drew her in his direction like some terrible wind-up soldier. Her face was caked with open sores, split and lacerated, bearded with dried blood.

Hands reaching for him, Kurta sighed, stuck the cigarette in his mouth and brought up the Ithaca. He jerked the trigger and she jerked as if she had been kicked. The round punched a hole in her chest and exploded out of her back, taking not only the fragments of her heart with it but sections of spinal vertebrae and a great, gushing quantity of fluid that splashed over the walls like an emptied pail.

He stood up, taking one last drag from his stale cigarette and flicking it away. It sizzled out in the fleshy wreckage of the woman's corpse. Without his helmet on, the stench was hot and putrid, unbearably gassy.

He saw two more coming and possibly a third.

And if his ears did not deceive him, more from the opposite direction. Well, it was high noon and time for a showdown. He figured this might be his last one, so he was going to go down shooting.

38

The Pole made it to the second floor, but when he got out into the corridor there were dozens and dozens of slugheads wandering about like shoppers gathering for a blue light special. Trying to shoot them all was silly. There was only one thing to do and that was to run. He charged past them, knocking more than a few aside in his mad grab at freedom. They clawed and tore at him and one little girl actually suctioned herself to his leg, but he bashed her with the butt of the riot gun. Another boy made a leap for him, and The Pole grabbed him in mid-air and used his own velocity to propel him over the railing where he splatted below.

The escalator.

It was the quickest way down. He knocked aside more sluggos, noticing with growing unease that dozens and dozens of them were pouring out of the stores. Most were walking. Some were crawling. Many others were writhing like worms.

He didn't want to know what that was about.

He blew the head off a large sluggo and tried to quickly jog down the escalator…but the steps were slick with blood and drainage, tissue and bones and body parts from Ex-Two. About half way down, as some sluggos from above followed in hot pursuit, he stepped into the husk of a corpse, lost his footing, and went bouncing down the rest of the way. The helmet protected his head from getting split open, but he twisted his ankle.

But even so, he moved rapidly once he got going.

God, the place was burning down. At the far end of the corridor, everything was on fire. Burning sluggos were stumbling about, dropping, trying to get up. When they couldn't, they crawled. The smoke was so thick he couldn't see anything. Only the filter of his helmet kept him from going to his knees. But it would be fouled before long.

He felt along the wall, gimping forward, searching for an EXIT sign. They were everywhere. He would find one soon. Just outside of Wet Seal, he paused, certain he heard footsteps keeping pace with him.

He waited.

He could hear the slugheads out there, some very close, screaming and howling in pain. Good. Let them all die. Let them all die horribly.

"As long as I don't die with them," he said to himself.

As he moved on, he was almost certain he was hearing those damn footsteps again. He followed the wall a little farther then, dammit, there they were. Every time he stopped, they stopped. It was getting under his skin. Worse, it was crawling right up his spine.

He kept trying to rationalize it in his mind.

His external mic was malfunctioning or just picking up a weird echo of his own footfalls. He was fatigued, ready to drop. He was practically melting in his hotsuit. The filter was probably going bad with all the damn smoke. All these things combined could have been messing with his head, making him giddy or delusional.

But you're not delusional, he told himself, *and you know it.*

He stopped again.

If it was just a sluggo—and what else could it be?—then why didn't it just show itself?

He could deal with that.

He could wrap his brain around that.

Trying to regulate his breathing, he realized he'd been standing there for some time, panicking, staring into the hot smoke that boiled around him in funneling clouds. He was seeing faces in it. Forms. Reaching figures. Horrible creeping shadows. All of them pressing in…tighter…and tighter…because *HE WAS ABOUT TO DIE—*

"Stop it!" he said.

He had to control his fear, master it, make it work for him as Kurta always said. That was it. Be smooth so nothing stuck to you. Be cool. Be ice. That was the thing because if he did that, then he'd walk out of this alive. He'd be the sole survivor and people at the bunker would—

Then a shape moved past him in the smoke. A hunched-over troll-like shadow that darted in, then retreated before he could really see it.

With a cry, he fired into the smoke.

Something shrieked with a high-pitched wailing.

Got you.

He hobbled away from the wall. He was going to put this fucker down for good, blow his or her ass out through the top of their head.

A figure jumped out at him—a crooked-backed woman whose upper body was a glistening mass of blood. He couldn't see much of her face through her tangled grease-clotted hair, but he could see her eyes and they were like black bullet holes.

She actually moved so quickly that she managed to get her rat-like paws on the barrel of the Ithaca about the same time he pulled the trigger, vaporizing her chest and dropping her just as fast.

But there were others.

The gunshots had drawn them.

They came vaulting out of the smoke, deranged and screaming, demonic things who attacked from every side. He got off two more rounds before the riot gun was ripped from his hands. He tried to draw his Colt Python and something struck his wrist with a devastating impact. He heard the bone snap and a jolt of white-hot pain went right up his arm.

As he cried out in agony, he saw one of them—*a teenage kid, a fucking teenage kid*—standing there with a baseball bat which he'd probably liberated from the display over at Pro Image.

By then, the others had hold of him.

He thrashed wildly, trying to break free, but it was just no good.

The bat came down again, and this time it hit his face bubble, leaving a broad white scratch in the Acrylite glass. It came down again and again, spider-webbing the glass with cracks and jarring The Pole nearly senseless.

Then they all got in on the act, kicking and stomping him, punching-in ribs and fracturing his right arm. One of them—a child—seized his twisted ankle in her teeth, biting down with punishing force on the torn, swollen tissues.

As he screamed with raw terror and pain, they were pummeling him. They had his legs and arms and they were trying to pull him apart. With the fractured and broken bones, it was sheer agony.

In his mind, a voice screamed, *Help me! Oh Jesus Christ, somebody help me! Get them off me! Don't let me go out like this! DON'T LET ME FUCKING DIE LIKE THIS!*

His helmet was yanked from his head and the sluggos squealed with delight. They jumped and chattered, snarled and snapped their teeth like blood-hungry baboons. Faces that were blistered and peeled, eyeless and ulcerated, cracked open and suppurating, pressed into his own. A girl with a face like a soft, rotten apple squirmed through the mass of arms and grinning faces, biting off the tip of his nose.

His suit was torn open and they were scratching and gouging him with ragged, filthy nails, peeling him like an onion as he went in and out of consciousness. He came to in a blood-spattered reality where red-stained faces bit and tore, blinking and moaning as he rode wave after wave of agony.

One of them yanked out a pink coil of intestine.

By then, it couldn't rightly be said that he was sane. The sluggos were like sharks hitting bloody meat. He felt as if everything inside him had gone liquid and was leaking from the many holes in his body.

And through the red mist, he saw a form in a filthy Tyvek suit and helmet step forward. The others fell out of his way and those that didn't, he cast aside. The Pole couldn't be sure by that point of what he was seeing...it was nightmare, it was phantasm, it was dream, delusions brought about by his life force ebbing.

Yet...

An exterminator with an American flag sticker on his blood-speckled helmet. That could only mean—

"MOONEY!" he cried out with the last of his strength. "HELP ME FOR GODSAKE! THEY'RE KILLING ME! THEY'RE FUCKING TEARING ME APART!"

And then Mooney, oh dear sweet God, Mooney was hovering over him and the others were watching. There was something wrong about that, but as his life fizzled out, The Pole could no longer reason or think. He could only accept.

Accept what his bleary eyes showed him.

And what they showed him was literally a horror beyond comprehension.

Mooney brought his helmet six or seven inches from The Pole's face and beyond the bubble there was nothing human.

Just an undulant fleshy mass. In his madness, The Pole was certain he was looking at thousands of grave worms in a fish bowl but what it was, of course, was a convulsive, squirming mass of flukes that multiplied and expanded until the face bubble popped free from internal pressure.

The flukes came gushing out in a surging tide of slime like maggots bursting from the skull of a road-struck collie.

The Pole drowned in them.

They wriggled over his eyes and pushed up his nostrils and filled his mouth and throat like wormy, moist suet.

It was an ugly death.

Thankfully, he was dead before they began tunneling into his brain.

39

They seemed to come from everywhere and Kurta met them, knocking them down like ducks in a fairground shooting gallery. He dropped eight of them with his Ithaca and then drew his Colt Python and killed six more.

But there were others.

There were always others.

Their voices filled the passage with insane shrieking and gibbering as they charged in at him. All he had left was his knife, one grenade, and the empty Ithaca. He had more shells, but they would have thoroughly gutted him by the time he even loaded a few.

They came for him and he went into a wild killing frenzy, swinging the riot gun like a club, shattering bones, smashing faces, and splitting heads.

And when that was taken away from him, he went at it bare-fisted, punching and kicking, knocking them out of his way and throwing them into each other and generally creating confusion that was lit by the fading lights of his helmet on the floor.

A screaming woman got her hands on his head and made to bite him in the face. He kneed her in the stomach and head-butted her, turned and punched the lights out of a man whose face was spongy beneath Kurta's fist. Then two of them grabbed him. He stomped a third with a kick, slid free, and when a large man seized him, Kurta did the only thing he could think of—he reached down with clawing fingers and tore open the man's slug-sack, ripping the slimy monstrosity from its womb and dashing it against the wall.

The guy went down as if someone had unplugged him.

Kurta did it three more times with like results. Then he charged into a pack of them, punching and kicking, slashing their slug-sacks with his knife and breaking free.

By then, of course, West was dead.

They had ripped him to pieces and were feeding on him.

Kurta ran down to the end of the passage with the pack hot on his trail. He cut to the left and then to the right again.

Suddenly, he saw light.

Just a sliver of it.

He poured on the steam until he reached it. There was a ladder set into the wall and he climbed it, gasping and panting. It was one of the access hatches that West had told him about.

This was it!

He pressed up on it, but it wouldn't move.

Feel around, dummy, feel around. There's gotta be a latch.

The pack was bearing down on him, screeching and slavering. This was it. He either got out now or he was never getting out. Dammit! Where was that fucking latch?

There.

He felt it.

But he couldn't get it to work.

He pulled out his cigarette lighter and flicked it. Sure, it was like a deadbolt. He pulled the bolt back and flipped the catch. This was it. With everything he had, he pushed the hatch up and it opened, clattering on its hinges to the sidewalk.

He pulled himself up and out.

Below, the sluggos filled the passage.

He pulled the pin on his last grenade and gave it to them, running like hell across the lot towards the APC. There was a thundering explosion and a chorus of screaming, but he didn't dare look back to see what had happened.

He raced across the lot, climbed up into the APC and slid behind the wheel, locking everything down. Then and only then did he allow himself time to breathe. He saw sluggos wandering about in the lot, but he had no fear of them now. He got a bottle of water and some beef jerky from the back.

As he replenished himself, he watched the sun sink away and darkness claim the land.

Okay, okay.

Time to go home. Time to go fucking home.

He turned over the APC and turned on the headlights. There was a long drive ahead of him and he knew he would be thinking about the kid, but he steeled himself because West was not the first friend he had lost.

Lighting a cigarette, he pulled the APC out of the lot and headed for the bunker.

40

Five miles out, he started to worry.

It was a very dark night and the only illumination came from the twin beams of the APC's headlights. By that point, he should have been able to see the lights in the bunker towers. They should have been shining like beacons. They were always manned and particularly at night. It wasn't, of course, like the old days when you had lit-up buildings and streetlights and all the rest. Now there was nothing but the moon and stars. The lights of the bunker, the tower, and security fence should have been visible for miles.

Tonight, they just weren't there and that set Kurta's skin to crawling.

He got on the radio again. "This is Kurta from Ex-Three. I'm coming in. Please respond."

He repeated the message four times over the next five minutes.

There was nothing but static out there.

Not good at all. In fact, it was downright scary. The most awful scenarios began to play through his mind.

Three miles out, he tried the radio again.

Then a mile out.

By the time he approached the berms outside the fence and could see the black and silent towers rising against the stars, he began to feel hollow inside. This was not just bad; it had all the makings of a tragedy.

He tried the radio one last time even though he knew it was pointless. If the guards in the towers hadn't challenged him by then, they weren't going to.

His paranoia told him to stay in the APC until first light. No sense poking around out there in the darkness and walking into an ambush or a nest of slugheads. There was plenty of room to bunk down in the back, food and water and weapons…why risk it?

Because those people in there were my friends, he thought then. *At least some of them. They might need help.*

"And there are children in there," he said in a low hurting voice.

He clicked on the lights in the back. If he was going to do this, he was going to do it right. He stripped out of his filthy biosuit and stuffed it in a plastic containment bag along with his gloves and underclothes. Standing there naked, he sprayed himself down with aerosol wormicide that smelled awful. He pulled on a fresh pair of camo fatigues from the locker. He grabbed an M4 with a tactical light bracketed to it and three extra magazines. He took a flashlight and three road flares. He would have liked some NVGs or grenades, but there were none. Lastly, he strapped on his knife and Colt Python.

Then it was time to see what this was all about.

41

He swallowed some Benzedrine to keep his edge and dropped the ramp on the APC.

He ran out, cutting between the berms. He circled far around the compound until he found the secondary gate which was chained and locked shut. He chose it because there was no barbed wire atop it. He scrambled up and over. He crossed the blacktop at a jog, expecting he knew not what.

Lots of things could have happened, the way he was figuring it.

Marauders could have gotten in and wasted everyone for the food, weapons, and other supplies stockpiled there. A slim possibility but conceivable. There could have been an armed overthrow from a group within the bunker. Again, a slim possibility but maybe. Slugheads could have overwhelmed everyone. Unlikely with the safeguards in place and the fact that the gates were all still locked. Lastly, there could have been some kind of freak slug outbreak. Things like that had happened at other bunkers. In a matter of hours, everyone could have been slugified.

When Kurta reached the entrance, he keyed in at the pad. All the exterminators had an emergency pin to be used only in the most dire circumstances.

Like this, he thought.

The door opened and he went in. It hissed shut behind him and locked. Silent alarms should have been tripped in three separate locations. Security people should have been bearing down on him by now.

But he heard nothing.

The silence remained unbroken.

He was more certain of it now than ever: everyone in the bunker was dead.

42

He moved quickly down the dark corridor, heading for the central hub. Someone was always there monitoring the outside security cameras. It was one of the locations where the silent alarm would have been triggered. As he approached it, his light bobbing up and down and casting threatening shadows over the walls, he could see the flashing red light on the console.

He disarmed it, then clicked on the lights in the hub.

"Shit," he said.

He saw two bodies, then a third and a fourth. A teenage boy, two women and a toddler sprawled in pools of drying blood. Without his helmet filtering the stink of blood and death, the smell made him feel more than a little green in the guts. They all died from the same sort of wound—the crowns of their skulls were split open from the hairline to the backs of their heads.

As grisly as it was, he had to get in closer and see.

It was important and he knew it.

Putting the tactical light of his M4 on each cleaved head, it looked as if they had been split open by something like an axe.

He thought: *An axe murderer? A hatchet killer?*

No, it was just too farfetched.

It couldn't be anything that simple.

Not now.

Not with the madhouse the world had become.

"What then?" he whispered.

He crouched down, putting his light right in the wounds. He examined them carefully and what he found made him even more sick than he already was.

Their brains were missing.

There was gore and strands of tissue in the skulls, but nothing else. Someone or some*thing* had licked them clean as soup bowls.

Kurta stood up slowly.

His mouth was dry and his heart was pounding. He went over to the console. His hand was shaking so badly he could barely thumb the intercom.

"This is Kurta from Ex-Three. I'm in the hub," he said, his voice echoing up and down the corridors, cutting the heavy, deadly silence. "If anyone's alive, answer me now or get to the hub. You've got ten minutes. After that, I'll kill anyone I find."

He sat down on the console desk and lit a cigarette, listening—and hoping—for the sound of footsteps. He was hearing things out there now, but they were not the sound of human feet.

Smoking, he waited.

And waited.

43

He gave it ten minutes, chain-smoking and feeling something loose shift inside him. The tension was nearly unbearable. Then it was time.

He began systematically searching the first floor, turning on lights as he went. He found more bodies. In fact, he founds lots of bodies and all of them had died the same way with their skulls ripped open. He counted twenty-three corpses. Most of the main living space was on the first floor—the kitchen and dining room, the infirmary, the rec rooms, the gym, as well as the greenhouses where they grew fresh vegetables and fruits.

He found bodies everywhere.

All of them missing their brains.

What troubled him was that despite the horrific head wounds, they all had the same peaceful, soporific look on their faces as if they hadn't felt a thing. That more than anything else made him suspect the slugs with their abundant pharmacies.

But slugs didn't have the equipment to split heads nor did they feed on brains. Their flukes did, but slowly, very slowly.

He walked from room to room, finding more bodies.

Place is a fucking morgue.

He saw too many faces he recognized and it pained him. He knew that eventually he was going to find Lisa Hilsson and it was going to hurt because he still had feelings for her.

You had a hell of way of showing it.

Now and again, he found some blood trails over the floors, smears that went out doorways and sometimes right up the walls.

Standing outside the greenhouse door (where he found five bodies), he lit a cigarette and tried to get his nerves in order. He was shaking. This was a new terror and he did not know what form it would take. That was the worst part. It was what kept him shivering and trembling.

What the fuck is this about? What the hell happened here?

Questions without answers.

Once he had been through the first floor twice and was no closer to any answers, it was time to go below. There were two more levels. One held the sleeping quarters, machine shops, and generator room. The one beneath that was where the lab was and where Major Trucks' digs were. Dr. Dewarvis and his people were down there. It was also where the supply rooms were.

As he made for the stairway which was down near the kitchen, he heard a scratching noise from the corridor he had just left. Wiping cold sweat from his face, Kurta went over there and saw…nothing.

But he knew he had heard it.

A scratching like fingernails on a door.

He waited for a time, but he never heard it again. Finally, he went through the door and down the stairs to see what he could find. All the way, something inside him—cold fear and instinct—told him to turn back, to leave this alone. To get back out to the APC and get out of there.

But he knew he couldn't.

That's not who and what he was.

He had to find out even if it killed him.

When he came through the door, he found more bodies right away. There were so many that he had to step over them. He found them in bed, on the floor, sitting in chairs, and sprawled in doorways. And they all had that serene, passive look on their faces. Something which was in great contrast to the gore that had dripped down their faces.

He found Lisa in her room. Both she and her daughter were dead like the others. There was nothing to do or say. He closed the door quietly, something breaking inside him. A few doors down, he found Daniella Creed in bed. Amazingly, she was alone. Naked, her charms on full display, she was smiling, her head split like a gourd.

Out in the corridor, he heard the scratching again.

In fact, he heard quite a bit of it.

He was about to find out what this was about and he knew it.

44

The scratching became a flurry of noise that came from every quarter.

The M4 held high, Kurta followed the corridor to the end, turning left past the stairs that led below and walking over towards the library and its adjoining rooms where the kids were schooled.

As he reached for the library door, the scratching stopped.

Just like that.

He hesitated, unsure, the sudden silence probably the loudest thing he had ever heard.

Fuck this.

He opened the door and stepped inside, fumbling about for the light switch. In those three or four seconds of darkness before he found the switches, nothing lighting up all the grim stacks but the light on his rifle, he had never been so completely afraid.

It was a special sort of fear.

The oldest and most debilitating fear man had ever known: the fear of the unknown. Nothing could hold a candle to it.

The lights chased away most of the shadows, but not those in his own head that lurked at the very edge of reason.

The library was no different than any other—there were reading tables and nooks, aisles and aisles of books, a children's area at the back. The only thing truly unique about it were the corpses slumped in chairs or sprawled on the floor where they had fallen, their heads laid open, blood and gray matter dribbled down their faces.

As he passed by a group of them, a woman fell over on the sofa, her face landing squarely in the lap of the man next to her. Under any other circumstances, it might have been funny how she face-planted so perfectly in his crotch. The moony grin on the man's face only accentuated the situation.

But it wasn't funny.

In fact, when it happened, Kurta jumped. It forced a strangled cry from his throat. And it didn't help that at her current angle, the fluorescent light overhead revealed the void of her emptied skull.

Then something fell.

Several things fell.

They thudded loudly to the floor. He tracked them to their source: the aisles of books. In the second row, three books were on the floor, having fallen from the highest shelf. One of them landed with its cover facing up: *In a Lonely Place* by Dorothy B. Hughes.

"Who's there?" Kurta called out, knowing someone was. He could feel their presence. It was heavy in the air.

Something moved behind him.

A few more books fell.

This time, however, he saw something move and fired in its general direction. Several books were ripped apart by the rounds, but nothing else. As fragmented pages drifted down around him like snowflakes, he turned and ran down the aisle and into the next.

It was here. I know it was here.

He stood there, breathing hard.

Something wet struck his face. It was cold, yet it burned. He wiped it away with a moan of disgust. It wasn't blood. It was brownish, nearly black, and it was slushy.

Another droplet fell and struck his shoulder.
It was coming from the clean air vent above.
Something was up there.

45

Kurta stepped away.

The vent was about three feet wide by maybe a foot in height. What the hell could possibly be up there? Not a man surely. Slug? Creeper?

Feeling hemmed in, he moved quickly back into the open where he'd have more maneuvering room if it came down to it.

He almost stepped on one of them.

A creeper.

It was wide in front and slender and wormy in the rear like the others. A bright glossy red, it was segmented and horribly centipede-like. It had the same tentacle-like appendages and slithering mouthparts.

That much was the same.

But what was different was that it was much larger, easily three feet in length. It seemed broader, thicker, more powerful looking. Like others he had seen, when it breathed it expanded like a bag of gas, mouth opening wide with each breath. But unlike them, its hollow tongue jutted out, wiggling in the air like that of a python. Not only that, but he could see a hook protruding from the upper jaw. It looked sharp and deadly like an ice pick.

As he made to open up on the thing, something moved behind him.

Another big creeper.

A *mega*creeper, for lack of a better word.

As it sucked in air, it inflated to twice its normal size, the mouth dilating and revealing the ribbed expanse of its throat. Its tongue tasted the air, that hook sliding from the gums.

And something more.

A fluttering diaphanous membrane that was frilly and pink extended from its sides and it *flew* through the air, gliding like a flying squirrel.

Kurta ducked and it missed his head by less than a foot. It looked like it would crash right into one of the bookcases, but it didn't. At the last moment, it veered off, spreading out and sticking to the wall like a thrown spitball. It clung there, vibrating. Its segments rasped together. Its hook scratched the paint, leaving furrows.

The other one on the floor launched itself and he drilled it with a three-round burst, knocking it against one of the tables. Torn and squeaking, it crawled a few feet, leaking a shiny purple-brown blood, then went still.

Another one launched itself from atop a shelf of books. Two more crawled from behind the sofa. Kurta darted away, bumping into a chair and overturning its corpse to the floor.

He shot another in midair, ripping it in half, splashing its blood over the serene faces of several cadavers.

They were everywhere now.

They crept up the walls and flew through the air and wriggled over the floor. And he saw why. As he'd suspected, they were coming out of the clean air vent in numbers.

The vents would have given them access to the entire bunker. That's what must have happened to everyone.

He ran, jumping and ducking, firing wherever he saw motion, killing creepers and ripping holes in the walls and perforating seated corpses.

He reached the door as another flew out at him.

He slammed it shut, and the creeper attached itself to the glass panel of the door like a snail to the side of an aquarium. Its underbelly was a shocking white, legs squirming. It held on by a vertical row of sucker-like knobs that he was willing to bet were designed to cling to prey and never let go. The knobs looked like flabby white lips, pulsating as if they were kissing the glass.

Out in the corridor, there were more of them.

He burned through the rest of his magazine and then another as they converged on him. They were thick on the floors, the walls, even the ceiling. He blasted them to worming fragments and painted the walls with their fluids.

Still more came.

There was just no way he could hold out alone.

He cut down another corridor, wasted two more creepers, and then another came seemingly out of nowhere, flying right at his face and he put up an arm to block it. It hit with incredible force, knocking him to the floor and making him drop the M4. Up close like that, it was a real horror. It clung to his arm by its suckers, its tentacle legs wrapping around his arm. He saw the mouth open and the hook come sliding out.

He pulled his .357 and drilled it with two shots, killing it. He tore it off his arm and the suckers broke free with a *pop-pop-pop* sound. He tossed its loathsome weight to the floor, and just as he had, another creeper tried to drop on him from the ceiling. He got out of its way, blew it apart, and another came sailing towards him. He caught it with a glancing shot that tore its side open, sending it careening into the wall. It hit the floor, bubbling out gouts of that weird blood that spattered in all directions.

Enough of this shit.

He grabbed up his M4 as more creepers showed. Retracing his steps, he took the first egress he could find which was the stairway to the lower level, the biocontainment level.

You sure you want to go down there?

But he was.

If he wanted answers to this nightmare, then that's where they would be.

46

Guiding himself by the light on his rifle, Kurta went down the first flight of stairs, banked to the right and went down another set.

As he keyed himself through the door and stepped into the corridor, another megacreeper shot out at him. He gave it a three-round burst dead on and it dropped flopping to the floor. He found the light switches and lit up the place.

He saw no more creepers.

He knew if he went to the left, it would take him to Major Trucks' office and quarters. Down there is also where Dr. Dewarvis and his crew had their digs. He saw very little of them. They spent most of their time in the bio lab, working on ways to eradicate the slugs. At least, that's what the official line was coming down from Trucks. What they were really doing was anyone's guess because no one was really allowed in there.

And maybe, just maybe, Kurta thought, *there was a very good reason for that.*

He didn't bother going to check out any of the offices or Trucks' hangout; he had no doubt whatsoever that everyone was dead. He went right to the bio lab. He'd been wondering how he would get in there because you needed key cards to access the doors, but he saw that wasn't a problem. The outer hatch was held open because there was a dead guy caught between it and the jam. One of Dewarvis' flunkies in a lab coat.

He stepped over the corpse, scanning about quickly, looking for creepers and seeing none.

The labs consisted of five interconnected rooms, all of which were quite large. He'd never actually been in there before. If he was looking for a clue, some evidence to explain what was going on, he wasn't going to find it. That much was obvious.

The place was trashed.

Desks and workstations were overturned, equipment shattered on the floor amongst human remains. The stench in there was ungodly. He stepped carefully over the mess, everything from IV bags and plastic tubing to laptop computers and surgical instruments. Drug cabinets were overturned. Digital microscopes dashed against the walls. He saw stainless steel tables with drains in them that were dark with old, crusty stains. Incineration units. Scattered bones. One of the few things still standing were a series of glass laboratory vats that held pickled specimens—wigglers, slugs, creepers, even several of the megacreepers.

He passed into another of the rooms, and this one held what looked like Plexiglas-enclosed containment cells. There was nothing in there but stains and bits of carrion.

He thought: *If you had to use your imagination, you could say that what was in those cells escaped or was allowed to escape.*

But that seemed too simple, way too simple. He was almost certain there was more to it than that.

He walked into another of the labs. He recognized what he thought was an electron microscope. Other than that, more of the same—computers and papers, instruments and odd-looking machinery smashed on the floor. There was also a very large containment cell. Its walls and ceiling and floor were covered with a putrefying black rot.

162

"Eggs," a voice said.

Kurta nearly jumped out of his skin.

He whirled around with the M4 and saw a very bedraggled-looking Major Trucks standing there. He wore a white Tyvek suit that was filthy with bloodstains and black smears. He looked thirty years older than the last time he had seen him.

"Hello, Kurt," he said.

His intensity was gone as was his characteristic volume. He looked…emptied, shrunken.

"What happened here?" Kurta asked him.

Trucks found a chair and settled into it. "What you see here is the bad ending to what could have been a very good idea."

Kurta just stared at him. "What are you talking about?"

"Sit down and I'll tell you."

Kurta shoved some folders off a desk and sat there. He lit a cigarette but did not set aside his carbine. He wasn't that comfortable with the situation.

Trucks sighed. "You see, Kurt, we never could figure out the origin of the slugs other than to assume—as so many did—that it was Mother Nature kicking us in the nuts for abusing the fine, lush green world she gave us. Maybe, maybe not. Regardless, we knew something had to be done. If the human race was to survive, the slugs had to be eradicated. Hence, this bunker. You know what its function was during the Cold War so there's no point in my going into that. As the slug menace increased and government after government was teetering on the edge of complete destruction as their populations became parasitized, the CDC, empowered by Homeland Security, stepped in. Along with WHO, these bunkers were reclaimed and refitted for a very different purpose than they had originally been designed for."

Kurta waited. "And what was that?"

"Some twenty bunkers were established in this country and some sixty others across the globe. Their purpose was to establish self-supporting communities that could thrive in relative safety and security," Trucks explained. "All of which would support the greater agenda which was bioengineering. These labs here are similar to the ones that every bunker contained and their purpose was recombinant DNA research."

"Genetic engineering?"

Trucks nodded. "It was our only real weapon against the slugs. Dr. Dewarvis and his people were, in their own way, creating an antidote to the slugs. Via forced mutation and molecular cloning, they created what all creatures on Earth must have to keep their populations in check: a natural enemy. They, in effect, enhanced the creepers."

"And then they got out and killed everyone," Kurta said.

Trucks ignored that. "Do you know what oxytocin is?"

Kurta had read about it. "It's...I think they call it the love hormone."

Trucks explained that oxytocin was generated in the hypothalamus and was released during pair bonding, whether that was sexual activity, hugging, or a mother nursing her child. It stabilized emotions, creating feelings of trust and relaxation. "This new breed of creepers is born addicted to it, Kurt. Without it, they spiral into anxiety and violence and paranoia, attacking and killing one another. When a person is parasitized by a slug and its flukes enter the brain, they manufacture large amounts of oxytocin. Dangerous, addictive amounts of dopamine *and* oxytocin, in fact. The new creepers can sense it and they seek it out. Do you see what I'm saying?"

Kurta did. "The megacreepers would attack the sluggos, going after the oxytocin."

"Exactly! The brain tissue would give them the nutrition they required for their metabolism and the oxytocin they extracted from the sluggos' brains would feed their addiction."

Trucks told him that, statistically, the entire process would take about three to four weeks once a sufficient number of megacreepers were bred. They would be released in the city, anywhere there were concentrations of slugheads too large for the exterminators to handle. The slugs and their hosts would be eradicated by the megacreepers who would go after their brains. Once the slugheads were decimated, the megacreepers would suffer horrible withdrawals, attacking each other for oxytocin and eliminating their own populations. It was quite simple.

"After the feeding frenzy, we would have to be careful, of course, because the creepers would attack *anyone* with oxytocin in their brains, meaning uninfected human beings. We had that worked out, too. After another three to four weeks, they would have all been gone either from feeding on one another or complete neural collapse from oxytocin starvation. They not only want it psychologically, Kurt, they have to have it from a physiological standpoint. They can't function without it. They need it like we need iron in our blood."

"Then they got out," Kurta said, seeing no point in hiding his cynicism any longer.

Trucks shrugged. "It was Dewarvis. He lost control. He and his people were, effectively, junkies."

"What?"

Trucks led the way across the room to a locked cabinet. He opened it with a key. There were little baggies of brown powder lined up, labeled and tagged.

Kurta just stared at them. His mouth went dry. His hands shook. He felt a strange bottomless hunger inside himself. Here it was again, staring him in the face. "Heroin," he said. Even the word was sugar on his tongue.

"Yes.

"Dewarvis and his people were on junk?"

Trucks shrugged. "Crude, but true. They were using it regularly."

"Why?"

"Because the *megacreepers,* as you call them, cannot tolerate it," Trucks explained. "Opium, heroin, and morphine are all derived from the opium poppy. The creepers in any form, as well as their hosts and attendant flukes, are highly susceptible to opioid toxicity. Even the slightest amount can send them into devastating anaphylactic shock."

Kurta started giggling; he couldn't help himself. He had all he could do not to begin laughing uncontrollably. "The only way Dewarvis and the others could safely work with these things was being stoned. That's rich."

"And like most users, they needed more and more as the addiction cycle progressed," Trucks said. "After a time, they were like any junkies. They cared less and less about what they had created and how to exploit it than they did about getting another fix. They fucked up. They got loose and sloppy, because in their drug fugues, the creepers were no threat to them. They wouldn't even come near them. They were harmless. The creepers were, in effect, neutered."

"And that's how they got out and killed everyone in this fucking place?"

Trucks nodded. "The creepers got out, into the ventilation system, probably entering it out in the corridor away from the biocontainment area. It was like a super highway leading to every level and every room."

"Every corpse looked happy," Kurta said more to himself than to Trucks.

"Of course they did. The megacreepers didn't savagely attack them. It's not their way. Just like their slug form, they have the ability to spit living globules of psychotropic drugs at their victims."

Kurta had seen that plenty of times. The slugs, despite their slimy, shapeless appearance, could shoot those globs with unerring accuracy.

Trucks went on to say that the slugs that attached themselves to people and unleashed flukes into their nervous systems, were addicts of a sort. The dopamine response that the flukes controlled in their hosts' brains also fed the slugs, being that they were wired to their systems.

"So the slugs were addicts from the very first," Trucks said. "With that in mind, it's not so strange that the creepers of both varieties would be as well. Dewarvis was never certain of the exact mechanics of the creepers' opiate allergy, but when he discovered it, he used it."

"And it used him," Kurta said, understanding the politics of addiction very well.

Trucks stood up. "That's the nature of what we're dealing with. That's the secret I could never tell." He shook his head. "The point being, we should get out of here. You have an APC outside?"

"Yeah."

"Let's go then."

Let's go then. Still barking fucking orders.

Kurta just stood there, feeling the M4 in his hands. He despised Trucks. Maybe the original idea behind Dewarvis' research was feasible and had potential, but it had gotten way out of control. And Trucks knew it. He knew the boys in the lab were addicts, irresponsible and reckless…yet he had done nothing. He had left them in charge of a highly dangerous, highly unpredictable biological weapon.

Now all these people were dead.

Kurta felt a strong desire to kill him, but what was the point?

"Our best bet is a location in the country," Trucks explained. "Somewhere secluded with very few slugheads. My suggestion is that we leave the bunker wide open. Let the megacreepers escape and do what they were designed to do. In a month or so, we can come back. We just have to let things run their course."

Kurta figured it was probably the only logical thing to do, yet he had the worst desire to feed Trucks to the megacreepers. It was what he deserved for being involved with Dewarvis and his bullshit. Even with the world's population teetering on the edge, men like them were still trying to manipulate things. They just couldn't stop being power brokers and lords of the Earth.

As long as there were men, it would never change.

47

Kurta led the way out with his M4. He gave Trucks his .357 Python and they made it without incident up to the next level. And that's when things went bad.

The megacreepers were massing.

They had fed on every brain in the bunker, stuffing themselves on gray matter and siphoning off the oxytocin that they needed to survive.

Now, many hours later, they needed another fix.

Trucks wasn't kidding when he said they were addicts. By the time he and Kurta reached the upper level, the megacreepers attacked in numbers. Pushed into oxytocin starvation mode, they would do anything to get it.

Anything.

In less than ten minutes, Kurta had burned off the last of his ammunition. There were dozens and dozens of dead creepers lying about, many still twitching and bleeding, bubbling slime.

But for every one of those, there were dozens that were very healthy and very determined.

Kurta and Trucks were forced back into the stairwell leading to the lowest level. They had no choice. They barely got through the door.

As he moved down the steps, Trucks screamed.

One of them was hanging from the ceiling and it spat a glob at him, catching him on the throat. Within seconds, it was too late. He screamed...then he started to giggle. He sat down on the steps, a stupid, drunken look on his face.

"TRUCKS!" Kurta shouted.

No good.

The glob had taken root in him, juicing him with psychotropics. He sat there, giggling, his eyes glazed over. As Kurta watched helplessly, he pissed himself and began to hum songs under his breath. He did not even seem aware that there was anyone with him.

He was gone.

He was literally gone that fast.

When the megacreeper dropped on him, Kurta pulled his knife. He would slice it, cut it, peel it off Trucks, but in the end, he did nothing.

The megacreeper clung to the back of Trucks' neck. It made a content, murmuring sort of noise that sounded like a lazy grasshopper. It and Trucks were joined, part of something bigger than the sum of their parts. It opened its mouth, its gums—pink like raw hamburger—pulled back and that wicked-looking hook slid into view. It traced along Trucks' scalp until it found the location it desired. Then the hook or tooth or whatever it was pierced his forehead, punching right into his skull. It was drawn back slowly, very slowly, making a wet crunching sound that nearly sent Kurta running.

And if that was bad, once the crown of Trucks' head was laid open—he was still humming something under his breath that sounded oddly like an old Duran Duran song, blood running down his face in a spider web pattern—it got considerably worse.

The megacreeper's body convulsed and vomited something into the skull. There was a bubbling/hissing sound like Pop Rocks dissolving in someone's mouth. Then the hollow tongue slid into the skull and there began a most terrible, repulsive slurping as it ingested his softened brain matter, sucking it up like pudding.

Kurta couldn't take it.

He got the hell out of there.

He made it out into the corridor, ducking a megacreeper and reaching the biocontainment area. The creatures started coming through the door right away, inching up the walls and over the ceiling.

Within thirty seconds, there were fifteen or twenty of them.

There was only one thing left to do and he knew it.

48

Over the next few days, wasted on junk, but feeling so good, hell yes, so very good, Kurta got down to work. He began dragging the bodies out of the bunker. Once he had thirty or forty of them out on the blacktop, he torched them with a flamethrower. The burnt smell was horrible, but it was better than the stink of carrion below.

He went on that way, snorting more and more heroin, knowing he was destroying himself as he had done before...yet, oddly empowered at the way the creepers feared him instead of the other way around.

By the end of the week, he gave up on it all.

He just didn't have the energy to drag bodies around and what was the difference anyway? They were just going to rot and what was he supposed to do about it?

Eating was a problem.

He was never hungry anymore and he was losing weight, so he had to remember to get something in his stomach now and again. The problem was all food started tasting bad. Every few days, when he started feeling really dizzy, he would eat a can of Spaghettios or something. He rarely could get it all down. He had to force himself to eat it in the first place.

His fourth day into it, he dragged up a mattress from downstairs and threw it in the rec room. That was enough for his needs.

He kept the generator going because he wanted lights and he liked to be able to watch TV. He started playing Sonic and

Mario again as he had when he was a teenager. It occupied most of his time.

There were things that needed doing, but he couldn't remember what they were most of the time so he gave up trying to.

He lived in the rec room.

He knew he was smelling bad and needed a shower, but he just couldn't bring himself to take one. It was easier to lay on the mattress and snort some skag, play video games and dream. His fatigues were filthy with bloodstains and corpse drainage from hauling the bodies out, but after a while, he stopped smelling them.

It was funny, he got to thinking, how he no longer had any purpose. He was of no use to himself or anyone else. Now that he was messed up on junk all the time, the creepers were no more threat than flies buzzing about.

Twice he drove the APC back into the city, getting on the loudspeaker and calling out for survivors. The only response he got was a bottle thrown from a rooftop. On one of these sojourns, he decided to test the slugheads. He found a pack of them and they came after him right away. He raised his Colt Python and prepared to do some killing.

They got within four feet of him, became confused, and moved off in the opposite direction. He followed them around, even reaching out and touching a woman. She cried out and ran off.

It would have been easy killing them.

But what was the point? It was no fun killing something that was no threat to you. There was no challenge in it. It was too much like shooting ducks.

After that, he never went back into the city again.

He laid on his mattress, playing video games.

At least at first. By the second week, he didn't have the energy for that either so he just laid there and watched the opening credits again and again. Sometimes he threw in a movie, but the voices drove him nuts because half the time he wasn't sure what they were talking about. It was better to watch with the sound off. It worked good with his dreams. They came even when he was awake now and, in the whirlpool of his mind, the dreams and what was on the TV were pretty much the same thing.

There was irony in the fact that what had originally destroyed his life was the only thing that could save it now.

But he no longer understood irony.

Somewhere during the second week, his highs really started bottoming out on him. He could barely get off anymore. That's when he went down to the infirmary for syringes.

After that, he got really wasted.

He lost all conception of time or how long he had been shooting up or what life had been like before. It didn't really matter. He knew he was a really pathetic, hopeless junkie by then, but it was hard to care.

Within a few weeks, he figured, he'd be out of heroin anyway.

The idea of that terrified him.

Part of him longed for it.

By then, most of the creepers were dead. They dissolved into mucky pools once decomposition set in. Trucks was right: in the end, they *had* attacked each other for oxytocin. They were pathetic, addicted things and Kurta found himself feeling sorry for them.

Junkies, nothing but worthless fucking junkies.

The idea of that made him giggle because all life forms in the final analysis were addicted to something.

He laid on his mattress, thinking his thoughts and dreaming his dreams, shooting up and zoning out, dirty and stinking, very often pissing himself.

One day—he did not know how long it had been, weeks, years maybe—he heard activity outside. It really meant nothing to him. Probably some sluggos sniffing around. *Come on in, my friends, fucking door is always open.* He kept hearing things, but he was far too drowsy to go see what it was. He zoned out and dreamed.

He woke some time later to the sound of voices.

What? What? Didn't I mute the volume?

When he opened his bloodshot eyes, he saw three figures standing there, watching him. They were wearing Tyvek suits and carried M4 carbines. Exterminators.

Hell was this?

Was it The Pole and West and Mooney all come back from the dead to haunt him? But no, these figures were real. He tried to talk but it had been so long that his voice was raspy, very crusty-sounding.

"Hey...hey...yoose guys there...hey..."

He pulled himself off the mattress, but he was so weak and so wrecked he went facedown. He pulled his head up and crawled in their direction. He noticed that he was not alone. There were three megacreepers crawling with him, scenting fresh supplies of oxytocin. Like him, they were weak and sluggish, an endangered species in the bunker.

"Wait...wait now," Kurta implored the figures. "This ain't...it ain't what it looks like..."

The figures opened up and a dozen rounds slammed into him, the final ones opening up his head like a can of soup and spilling its contents over the floor. He twitched a few times and went still.

The megacreepers were likewise killed.

"Hey, Spengler, is that him?" one of the exterminators asked.

"Yeah, that's Kurta," Spengler said, practically choking on his own hate. "I'd know that asshole anywhere."

One of them flipped Kurta's scrawny corpse over with his boot. "He don't even have a slug."

"So what?" Spengler said. "Fucking out of his head. Look at him. Filthy, stinking, living in his own waste…he's been asking for this a long time."

"Lucky we found you, Speng, or you'd be like him now."

Spengler grunted, but said nothing. What was there to say? The boys from Wright-Patterson found him curled up in one of the APCs two days after the mall burned to the ground. He was barely rational.

He looked down at Kurta's corpse.

The truly amazing thing, he noticed, was that it was smiling. Smiling the way Kurta never had in life. They dragged him outside along with the remains of about twenty others that were so decomposed they had to be bagged. Later, near sunset, they toasted the death pile of human and creeper remains.

Spengler stood there for a long time, watching it burn.

—The End—

CHECK OUT OTHER GREAT APOCALYPSE BOOKS

XY
by D.S. Lillico

An iron fortress protected by automated gun turrets is the only world Elsie has ever known.

When tragedy strikes, Elsie is forced to leave the sanctuary of her home and out into a brutal new world. A post-apocalyptic wasteland filled with savage mutants.

Hunted and alone Elsie stumbles into the care of a giant named Punch, but the world is now full of worse things than giants. Cannibals are starving, bandits are roaming and war is coming.

Elsie's arrival plunges the new-world further into darkness... and is there really something hidden inside of her?

SANCTUARY
by Ian Page

Deeta Nakshband, a Connecticut physician is attacked by a local surgeon while on duty in the hospital. Her friend, Janelle Jefferson, has similar experiences in Miami. Both of them become aware of an increasingly violent world as acts of isolated brutality escalate into civil unrest. They grapple with their paranoia as family members and coworkers become dangerously unpredictable. Worldwide, military units go rogue, war begins in Korea and cities implode as people slaughter each other in the streets. Martial law is declared in an attempt to maintain order. People are arrested, detainment camps are set up and interrogations end with tragic consequences as modern civilization crumbles. Deeta and Janelle band together with family friends and coworkers to save each other and find sanctuary.

CHECK OUT OTHER GREAT APOCALYPSE BOOKS

THE DEAD FAMILIAR
by J.D. McKenna

In the twilight hours of a failing world, one man seeks to bring his loved ones to safety. Jack Hightower: Marine, barkeep, and doomsday prepper. He knows of the coming calamity, and on the final night of an old world he seeks a new beginning.

This is the story of that night, the tale of how Jack and his survivor's colony in the north came to be.

DOMINION
by Doug Goodman

Dominion has been taken from man. Now, six friends must cross an apocalyptic wasteland dominated by a hell's menagerie of mega-fauna. Their middle-class suburban skills are no longer applicable to the world they live in. To find a safe haven in this world they will need to develop a new set of survival skills and fight the mutated denizens of the animal kingdom for every step of their terrifying journey.

 SEVERED**PRESS**

CHECK OUT OTHER GREAT APOCALYPSE BOOKS

WHITE OUT
by Eric Dimbleby

An apocalyptic snowstorm sweeps the globe. Experts predict this freak storm will be "The New Ice Age." Electricity is gone, as are all forms of communication and road travel. As each member of a divided family tries to survive in their own way, they must deal with a snow-driven madness that has gripped the underlying evil in the hearts of men. In an epic struggle to get home and reunite, they will find that terror lies around every snow drift... and even in their very own backyard.

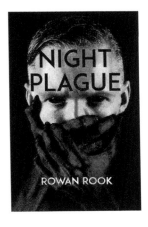

NIGHT PLAGUE
by Rowan Rook

Humankind will soon be extinct. A mysterious pandemic cut through two-thirds of the population in just four short years, and within another four, it will decimate everything – and everyone – left.

The last days are ticking by, relentless and ruthless, and the reclusive Mason Mild finds himself torn between a peaceful end and a brutal immortality. Between his hopeless, but comfortable days with his family, and something new...something violent and wild.

Have the fang marks above his heel dealt him an early demise or a second birth?

39726651R00108

Printed in Poland
by Amazon Fulfillment
Poland Sp. z o.o., Wrocław